THE CHAOS JAR

BLOOD MAGIC
BOOK FIVE

JT LAWRENCE

FIRE FINCH

FIRE FINCH

 Created with Vellum

ABOUT THE AUTHOR
JT LAWRENCE

JT Lawrence is a USA Today bestselling author of 30+ books, and a Kindle Unlimited All-Star. Mother to a menagerie of chaos, voracious reader, gin fan, and urban farmer.

*Stay up all night
with USA Today bestselling author
JT Lawrence.*

www.jt-lawrence.com

amazon.com/author/jtlawrence

tiktok.com/@stay_up_allnite

instagram.com/authorjtlawrence

facebook.com/JanitaTLawrence

x.com/stay_up_allnite

bookbub.com/authors/jt-lawrence

pinterest.com/stay_up_all_night

linkedin.com/in/janita-thiele-lawrence-56533610

SPECIAL THANKS

Immense gratitude to my readers
whose loyalty, support, and generous reviews
give me the courage to face the blank page
over and over again.

I wouldn't be able to do this without you.

I hope you enjoy this new magical adventure!

- Janita (JT Lawrence)

THE CHAOS JAR

BLOOD MAGIC BOOK 5

CHAPTER I

EARTH, AIR, WATER

T he new captain of the Scorpions yanked my
cuffed hands toward the door.

He was going to personally accompany me to
the Black Tower after his officers found the Council-
prohibited vial of voodoo serum, or *Spiritus Morbus*, in my
apartment. A man in uniform bagged up my wand and my
crossbow while another pushed a struggling Gizmo into a
police-issue animal carrier. The carrier was the epitome of
depression: a gray plastic cage. I hated seeing Gizmo's
little pink nose behind the door as it snapped shut. His
nervous eyes tracked the strangers as they invaded our
home.

Not satisfied with confiscating my mother's silver wand,
Musubarin stripped me of my bike-summoning ring, my
father's pentacle ring, the Belore Dragon's Eye amulet, the
silver bullet star charm from Darick, and Lou's djinn

stone. They all went into the same bag. I stood there, bereft.

Musubarin tugged at me again, and the silver handcuffs bit into my wrists.

"Come on," he said. "There's nothing left for you here."

My heart pounded.

Would this be the last time I ever saw my apartment?

I wasn't particularly attached to my material possessions, but I was attached to the ghost that haunted them. My body felt heavy, and sick with dread. I was completely vulnerable without my wand or weapon. I was barefoot, and I felt practically naked in my thin cotton *Rocking the Realm* T-shirt and sleep shorts.

"I'm in my pajamas," I said. "I need to change."

He shook his head. "No."

"Shoes, then," I said. "And a coat."

Tilexon didn't know my coat was magical, or he would have impounded it with the rest. He looked impatient, and then gave the officer standing behind me a tight nod. The cop went to my room and brought back my boots. Then, un-cuffing one wrist at a time, he helped me into my trench coat. I immediately felt fortified, and I thanked him.

"Put her in the car," said Musubarin, but I wouldn't budge until he understood the precariousness of the situation.

"Tilexon," I said. "You don't understand what's happening. It's not about me, or you. If we don't stop the Silvano Clan, the Realm is going to burn."

"I don't have time for your little conspiracy theories," he said.

"They already have the HighFire Crown," I said. "That's one of the three elemental fragments they need to ignite the fire that will destroy the Realm."

Musubarin sneered at me. "You're even crazier than I thought."

"Earth, air, water," I said. "When those fragments are brought back together the dark magic will catch fire and destroy everything."

"Can you actually hear yourself?" he asked. "You're certifiable."

"I know it sounds crackers," I said. "But I'm telling you it's true."

I think I did well by leaving out the part where my resident ghost had communicated this message to me by slamming the ancient red hardcover to the floor.

Musubarin sighed and crossed his arms. "What are these fragments?" he asked. "Where are they?"

"The book doesn't say."

"Ah." He was so patronizing I felt like kicking him in the toolbox again, but I restrained myself.

"You can't disseminate that kind of information," I said. "It would be too dangerous. They're too powerful. Everyone would be searching for them."

"I've had enough of your ridiculous distractions," snapped Musubarin. "We're leaving."

"I'll show you the book."

"The book?" he said. "I don't have time for this."

"It's right there." I gestured at my bookshelf, which was just a couple of steps away from where we were standing.

Tilexon sighed again, then snapped his fingers in an arrogant way. I strode over and grabbed the red book, memorizing the author's name as I did so.

Griffin Zolastaro.

It sounded more like a stage name for a magician than an academic who spent his life studying vampire lore.

With my back turned to the irate captain, I also managed to pull out Zeel's notebook, which I secretly slipped into my coat pocket. Zeel was the dark arts courier delivery man; a goblin who serviced the vendors at the EverShade night market. His book—which I had managed to snatch off him using my feral quick-and-dirty magic—was brimming with the names and addresses of hundreds of people who had bought Council-banned substances. It was, for someone like Tilexon, a veritable gold mine.

I turned and passed the captain the red hardcover, opened to the relevant page. He took it from me with a mildly disgusted look on his face, as if I had handed him a week-old taco.

"I wouldn't have believed it, either," I said. "But I've seen firsthand how potent the magic of the HighFire Crown is. And it seems to get more powerful each day."

I gestured at the plant that was in the process of swallowing my kitchen whole, and Tilexon blinked at me, then went back to the book. He flipped the pages and frowned.

"I'm pretty sure the Crown is the earth fragment," I said. "So we need to secure the air and water fragments, but I don't know what those are, or how to find them."

Not even Gizmo would be able to help me find them if I didn't know what I was looking for. The captain rubbed his lips and chin, and for a moment I thought he'd do the right thing. I thought he might see the big picture, remove my handcuffs, and perhaps even try to help me find the magical items we needed to stop Acheron and the Silvano Clan from decimating the Realm.

I was wrong.

CHAPTER 2
GLITTER & TRASH

Captain Musubarin pushed me roughly out the door of my apartment and into the mouth of the Swift. An officer accompanied us—the kind one who had helped me put my coat on—and as we dropped from the top of the tower to the basement, my stomach fell, too.

Tilexon pushed me into the back seat of his bullet-proof Scorpion-issue SUV and when he reached over me to click in my safety belt I looked away, out of the tinted window. It was too intimate a gesture for a man I despised, and I hated being so close to him and his freshly shaved skin that smelled of tea tree oil. The accompanying officer sat in the front passenger seat, with Gizmo in the animal carrier on his lap. Musubarin climbed in the driver's seat and slammed the door closed.

"What are you planning, Tilexon?" I asked. "What is your end game?"

"Justice," he said. "You, in prison."

"I don't deserve to be there. You know that."

"You flout the laws as if they don't apply to you," he said, his knuckle-bones showing white on the steering wheel. "You think you can do anything. Get away with anything. Well, I'm going to bring an end to that. You think you're a renegade—"

"The Realm needs renegades," I said.

"You think you're a renegade but really you're just a little girl who can't stay out of trouble."

Filius canis, I thought. What a son of a bitch. His words shouldn't have hurt me, but they did. Some people say I'm the best wizard detective in the city, but a small part of me will always be that scared little girl.

I sat there, fuming, and then realized I was wasting my time being angry. Thoughts of revenge would be a lot more constructive. I would escape Musubarin if it was the last thing I ever did, and he would die knowing that he could never have me. I knew that my slipperiness infuriated him. I grew up as a feral wizard in a mean city; one of the first things I learned was how to be difficult to pin down.

· · ·

WE STOPPED at a traffic light and I looked around. The Jozi streets looked post-apocalyptic; littered with burning waste and glinting with shattered panes of glass. Glitter and trash. The more disturbing thing was the look on the peoples' faces. There weren't too many pedestrians around, but the ones I saw had a horrible vacant expression on their faces. Before, they had been anxious, fearful, aggressive. Now all I saw were masks of indifference, as if they had been hypnotized into not caring. A woman with a torn floral-print dress was walking toward the SUV, her eyes unseeing. She got closer and closer, and the traffic light remained red.

"She doesn't see us," I said, and both of the men glanced back at me, then to where I was looking. The woman in the floral dress kept walking. I waved at her, but there was no sign of acknowledgment. Then there was a bump of body on metal as she walked straight into the side of the car, and melted down to the ground. The officer in the passenger seat clicked his safety belt off and opened his door, carefully putting Gizmo's cage on the floor in front of him. He jumped out of the vehicle.

"Ma'am?" He walked around to my side and helped the woman up. "Ma'am?" he said again, holding her limp body up and trying to look into her eyes, which he levered open with his fingers. That's when I saw him flinch, just a little, and he let go of her eyelids.

"What is it?" asked Tilexon. He was impatient to get going. Every minute that I wasn't locked up in a cell made him feel intensely uncomfortable. I stared at his neck, and saw that his body was as tense as a bowstring drawn back and ready to shoot.

"What is it?" asked Musubarin again, this time through clenched teeth. He had seen the man flinch, too.

"Nothing," lied the officer.

I knew he was lying, because I had seen it, too. The whites of the woman's eyes were bloodshot, and her irises were silver. The officer hoisted her body higher, and began to walk around the SUV. He opened the door opposite me and began easing the woman in. Her legs were dirty and bruised, and her ponytail was loose, close to falling out of its hair elastic altogether.

"Tshabalala," Musubarin said, grimacing. "What the hell do you think you're doing?"

Tshabalala met his gaze. "We can't just leave her here," he said.

I stared at the unconscious woman for the rest of the trip, trying to figure out what was wrong with her and the other people I had seen with the same blank faces. I could sense she was untouched and something that Lysander had said to me a few hours ago rang in my ears.

"When you blew up that lab it forced the Clan to think of a new strategy to recruit soldiers. A much more dangerous design."

Musubarin and Tshabalala tried to drop the woman off at a hospital that was on our way. Injured people milled around the entrance, but there was little point. The medical staff's parking lot was empty and the entrance doors were locked.

"Something terrible is going to happen," Lysander had said, right before I slammed the door in his face.

Moose ground the car's gears and kept driving.

ONCE WE ARRIVED AT HQ, Tshabalala radioed for assistance while Tilexon wrenched me out of the SUV.

"When's the next Onyx transfer van arriving?" I asked.

"Don't get smart," he snapped.

Of course, there would be no more transfers to the port. Not until the Ember Isles ferry was replaced, and it's not like you can get those shipped overnight from eBay. I wondered how he was planning on getting me to the Black Tower when the blown-up pieces of the ferry had drifted to the ocean floor.

"Sleeping with the fishes," Don Vito would have said.

There was a chopping sound in the air, and soon a large

black military helicopter was slicing the sky above us. It landed expertly on the top of the Scorpion HQ building.

"Best hurry up," said Musubarin. "Our lift is here."

CHAPTER 3
VIOLENT MAGIC

Captain Musubarin grabbed my arm and forced me into the building. Nothing about the man was gentle: he smashed through the double doors at the entrance and through the security turnstiles, slamming his access card against the sensor. When the receptionist greeted him, he just grunted in her direction. I hated the feel of his hot palm on my skin, hated that he was allowed to touch me just because of the badge pinned to his chest. Being unarmed—and in my pajamas—added to my sense of powerlessness.

I thought he'd take me right up to the top of the building and force me into the chopper, but instead he pressed the elevator button for level two, which is the floor I knew; the floor where Morgan's office was. The heavy metal doors closed and I looked Musubarin in the eye, trying to figure him out. Trying to find the source of his bitter hatred of me.

I mean, I know I'm not everyone's cup of tea—introverted, jaded, cynical, reckless, damaged, with a touch of crazy—but I didn't understand the depth and intensity of his dislike for me. From the beginning he had a chip on his shoulder the size of Gallanrock, and I didn't know why. There was no point in asking him. I had already figured out that he was as good at lying as he was at making women feel weak.

"Look at us," I said. "Again. Why are you always trying to get me alone in an elevator?"

"Don't flatter yourself," he sneered.

"I miss that troll glamour of yours," I said. "It was an improvement."

"Such a smart mouth, Knight," he said. "Do you kiss your pet weasel with that mouth?"

Tilexon mentioning Gizmo made my stomach flutter with fear.

"He's a ferret," I said in a softer voice. I didn't mind antagonizing Musubarin when my comfort was at stake, but I didn't want him to take his anger out on Gizmo.

"Ferret, weasel," he said. "It doesn't matter. Or, at least, it won't matter."

The flutter in my stomach turned into a fist.

"What do you mean?"

"What?" He feigned innocence. "I don't mean anything."

I swallowed hard. "Musubarin," I said, raising my voice. "What do you mean *it won't matter?*"

"What did you think would happen to it?" he said. "Did you think we'd let you take it along to the Black Tower?"

"I—"

"Do you have any idea what it's like there?" His eyes were burning into mine. "Do you think they allow *pets?*"

"I have friends who can look after him for me," I said. "The owner of *The Copper Cog and Ale.*"

Tilexon raised his eyebrows at me then shook his head as if he were pretending to be sorry. "Ah, shame. You haven't heard."

"I have heard. I know the Hammerskins have annexed the place."

"If, by *annex*, you mean *burn to the ground*, then, yes, *The Copper Cog* has been *annexed.*"

"No," I said, not breathing. "You're lying."

"Wish I was," he said. "It was a good little place. Good beer. Now it's all a blackened mess. We drove past it a few hours ago. It was still smoking."

I could feel my heart crumble in my chest.

"We had to send a team to investigate. Make sure those devious dwarfs weren't trying to grab the insurance money."

"The Fernaks would never do that. Ferra Fernak has more common decency in her little finger than you have in your entire body."

It was a cliché, I knew, but it was true.

"Besides, they'd never burn it down. *The Copper Cog* was everything to them."

It was everything to me, too.

My body jerked, as if it wanted to dash out of the building and rush to see Ferra. The elevator doors pinged, and Musubarin pulled me out and along the beige-carpeted passage.

"The inspector said it wasn't caused by arson, so you can relax. Your dwarf friends won't be going to jail any time soon. We're not charging the Hammerskins, either. Apparently you can't arrest someone for being stupid, which, personally, I think is a downright shame."

"The Hammerskins burnt it down?"

"Not on purpose. They left one of the gas stoves on while they were sleeping. Then someone woke up and lit a cigarette. As I said, you can't arrest them for being stupid. Besides, the orc who lit the cigarette got his punishment. They're still scraping bits of him off the floor."

"But you could arrest them for trespassing," I said. "For stealing land."

"Nope," said Musubarin. "Council mandate. We're to let the orcs govern themselves."

"Govern themselves?" I said. "That's like asking cats to herd themselves."

In theory, all the different species in the Realm do govern themselves, but the Council was always the highest power and would make sure it was done fairly and justly, and step in if necessary. Neo-Nazi orcs murdering Khargol loyalists and "annexing" private property was neither fair nor just.

Moose shrugged. "Orders from above."

WE REACHED THE CHARGE OFFICE, and Tilexon pushed me down into one of the grubby plastic chairs that lined the chipped wall.

"Sit," he commanded. "Stay."

He ambled up to the counter and began chatting to the officer there. I heard him say my name, and then he began to reel off the charges he was bringing against me. I tapped my foot. It was a long list. So long that if I were a male wizard I was sure I would have felt my beard growing.

When I heard him mention Gizmo I sat bolt upright and pricked up my ears.

"...animal handler. No need to take the thing away, he can just do it here. We've got facilities to dispose of the body."

I shot up. "Musubarin," I seethed. My insides were roiling with lava. "You wouldn't."

He turned around and looked at me with his ugly pursed lips. "Ms. Knight," he said. "I'd remind you to stay calm."

"Don't you dare." Despite not being armed, the fear and loathing I felt for the man was fizzing beneath my skin and making my fingertips tingle. "Don't you dare do anything to Gizmo!"

"Don't take it personally," he said. "It's Scorpion policy."

"Scorpion policy?" I asked. "Since when?"

"Since I became the boss," he said. "Now sit down, or you'll be sorry. And no more sudden movements. There are a lot of armed officers here. I wouldn't want you to be shot *accidentally*."

I didn't budge, and nor did my magic. It was coming off me in waves. I was ready to sling the mother of all *rumpis* spells at the wizard. I was going to the Ember Isles anyway, wasn't I? So I may as well make it count. Let them shoot me; let them fill me with lead. It would save them a helicopter ride.

"Tilexon," I said, my voice as calm as a dead man. "I won't let you do that."

The charge officer looked at us, her eyes wide. She knew that *faex* was going to go down.

"Shall I c-call someone?" she stuttered.

"Just call the animal handler, Sandra. As I instructed you to," Musubarin said. His gaze felt like ice cubes on my neck. "Tell him to bring the pentobarbital."

The charge officer picked up the phone, almost dropped it, then clutched it to her chest. She couldn't dial because her eyes were glued to us. She could feel the violent magic dancing in the air.

CHAPTER 4
ELECTRIC SMOKE

"Put down the phone, Sandra," I said.

Sandra clutched the phone receiver and gaped at us, unsure of what to do.

"I gave you instructions," Musubarin said to the charge officer, without taking his cold eyes off me. "Now follow them."

"Yes, detective," she said, then corrected herself. "C-captain."

She stared down at the buttons on the phone, but didn't move. She looked as if she had forgotten how to use the appliance. Then it seemed to come back to her, and she began to dial.

"Sandra," I said. "Put. The. Phone. Down."

She hesitated again, and Musubarin lost his temper. "Damn it!" he shouted, and I had the feeling he wanted to kick the wall. While he was temporarily distracted by his own short fuse, I stared at the receiver in Sandra's hand.

Rumpis! I thought. The phone blew, sending out a small silver explosion and a puff of electric smoke. Sandra screamed and hit the deck, as if I had bowled a Death Spell at her instead of just short-circuiting her phone. I heard boots moving swiftly, and the sharp metallic click of guns near my head.

I slowly raised my hands, showing I was handcuffed and unarmed. Half a dozen officers surrounded us.

"Jax!" said one of them, and I blinked and focused on someone at the back. She was wearing lipstick the color of a London Bus.

"Morgan!"

She holstered her gun and pushed thorough the other officers.

"It's all right," she said to them. "The situation is under control. Put your weapons away."

They didn't need to be told twice. They backed off, happy to return to the half-eaten sandwiches at their desks.

"Morgan," I said again. I was so relieved to see her. I wanted to throw my arms around her but I was jangling with metal cuffs and chains and it wouldn't have made for a very comfortable hug. I was carrying so much steel it would have made a metal detector explode.

She looked me up and down. "What the hell?"

"It's none of your business," said Tilexon. "Get back to work."

"He wants to kill Gizmo," I said. "Please help me. Please take him for me."

"Of course," she said. "Of course I'll take him. But what has happened—"

"It's too late," said Musubarin. "It's too late for you. And it's too late for your pet weasel."

He seemed like a caricature, then. A villain in a kids' film. *"It's too late for your pet weasel."* I mean, what self-respecting captain of a special ops team would actually say that out loud?

Morgan and I looked at him with all the contempt he deserved.

"Gizmo is not a weasel," said Morgan.

"Get back to work," he snarled. Then he directed his fury at the charge office counter again. "Sandra!" he yelled. "Sandra! Get that charge sheet wrapped up. Chopper's waiting."

Sandra, still looking a little shell-shocked, rose slowly from behind the desk. "Yes, sir," she said, and began to scribble with trembling hands on the clipboard that had my name on it.

"What happened to you?" Morgan whispered.

"Don't worry about me," I said. "Just get Gizmo. Please."

"Where is he?" she asked.

"Tshabalala took him to the forensics room," said Musubarin. "He's being held as possible evidence."

"Bullshit," Morgan said, hand on hip. "You're holding a ferret? Seriously? That's ridiculous, Musubarin, even for you."

"Just until the animal handler gets here," he said. "Then that particular piece of evidence can be destroyed."

My magic surged again. I swear, if I'd had a syringe of pentobarbital in my hand I would have plunged it into his small, stony heart.

"I can't get into that room," said Morgan, her face leached of color, which I was sure reflected mine. "I lost my access privileges after that disciplinary hearing."

If karma was ever deserving of her nickname, now was the time.

I was the one who had stolen Kim Smith's sworn statement out of Morgan's office. I was the one responsible for getting Morgan called into that disciplinary meeting. And now I would be the one responsible for Gizmo's death. I had to stop this from happening. I had to stop Tilexon. Sparks flew through me, my energy climbed. Magic was surging through my veins. This time I wouldn't just destroy the phone. I would destroy Tilexon. The world could thank me later.

"Stop," said Morgan to me. "Don't do it."

Her gentle words broke my concentration. I blinked and looked at her.

"Whatever you've done," she said, looking at my new Scorpion-issue silver jewelry, "I can help you. But if you kill Musubarin there will be no way out."

The magic simmered inside me. I knew she was right. I took a deep breath and tried to douse the flames I felt in my fingers and in my heart.

"Okay," I whispered to her. "Okay."

TILEXON PUSHED his greasy bangs out of his face. "I've told you already, Morgan. Get lost."

"No way," she said, folding her arms. "I'm not going anywhere. I'm not leaving Jacquelyn with a man I don't trust."

"I'm warning you, Detective," he said. "Get back to work or face the consequences of another disciplinary meeting."

"Oh, Moose," she said, rolling her eyes. "Bite me."

If Gizmo's life hadn't been at stake, I would have laughed. But as it stood, not even a joke the size of Musubarin could get me to crack a smile.

"Is that paperwork ready?" he asked the charge officer.

"Almost," she said. "Waiting for the rubber stamp. It shouldn't take long, but Control messaged me to say the pilot's taking a break."

Musubarin looked at me and then grabbed my arm again the way he was so fond of doing, forcing his sharp fingertips into my flesh. "You can wait in SubT."

My anxiety spiked. I did not want to wait in the subterranean holding cells. I could think of at least a thousand horrible things I'd rather do than get locked into one of those dungeon cells.

"No," said Morgan, standing in our way. "SubT is full. In fact, it's more than full. It's overcrowded, which is against regulation. There's no more space for anyone."

"Bull," spat Tilexon. "SubT has never been full."

"SubT has never been full because we've never been on the brink of civil war. Have you even been outside in the last forty-eight hours? Or have you been so obsessed with Jacquelyn that everything else just fades into the background for you? We're rounding up Hammerskins and goblins on every callout. Murder, rape, torture, arson, theft. It's like they've all gone crazy out there."

That made me think of the untouched woman we had seen on our way to the headquarters, the one who walked straight into the SUV and lost consciousness. The orcs and goblins weren't the only creatures acting strangely.

"If you had a shred of integrity," said Morgan, "You'd let this wizard go and you'd go after some really dangerous people. Raguk Magra, for one."

Musubarin guffawed. "Raguk Magra."

Raguk Magra was the commander of the Hammerskins, the kingpin, and he ate wizards like Tilexon for breakfast.

"What's wrong, Moose?" she asked. "Are you scared?"

"You don't *go after* Raguk Magra," he said. "Magra is ensconced at Alcazar. No one gets in there. It's all tangled up in amateur orc enchantment magic and razor wire."

The Hammerskins' magic may be amateur, but their battle skills were on fleek. Automatic guns, shivs, swords, flails, bows and arrows. Anyone who dared cross the line of that fortress would be instantly quilled like a porcupine. And that's if they were wearing their lucky underpants.

The stories of what the Neo-Nazis were doing to their sworn enemies—i.e., whoever dared glance in their general direction—were horrific and terrifying; the stuff urban legends were made of. They had made their mission clear a few days before when they had sawed off The Boss's head and stuck it on a spike outside his residence.

Anyone tied to the Khargol *familia* in any way would be slaughtered and displayed; men, women, and children alike. There were stories of brutal torture on the Forage newsfeed with headlines so savage you had to look away. Stories that made ancient Tang dynasty *lingchi* executioners look cuddly in comparison.

No, there was no way Tilexon would be chasing after that particular death wish. Not when he had someone like me to bully.

"The Realm is burning," said Morgan. "You need to be out there, leading the troops. They need direction. They need a strategy, or they'll just be cut down."

"I have an idea," said Musubarin. "How about: you do your job, and I'll do mine."

"I am doing my job, you—"

"That V-Cult case," he said, his eyes looking a bit crazy. "That V-Cult case is still very much unsolved."

"It's not a priority at the moment," she said.

"Almost a dozen women killed in cold blood," he said. "A serial killer cult on the loose. And you say it's not a priority?"

"More people are dying on the streets—"

"All I'm hearing are excuses," he said. "Excuses as to why a washed out lady cop can't solve her cases anymore."

"Filius canis," I said, my magic boiling in my chest.

Morgan clenched and unclenched her fists, but remained calm.

"Now, I'm going to say it again," said Tilexon. "You do your little job, and I will do mine."

It looked like Morgan's head was going to explode. A vein in her temple throbbed as if it wanted to break free and strangle the asshat standing in front of her.

"Now, as lovely as it's been, standing around chatting, I have work to do." He grabbed my arm again and wrenched me forward, in the direction of the stairway that snaked down to the dungeon cells.

Morgan blocked our way again. "No," she said. "I'm not letting you lock her up with those miscreants, no way."

I thought of the gray-skinned goblin and shuddered. My short experience with him had already fueled nightmares.

"Get out of my way, Morgan," said Musubarin. He was seething and looked ready to lash out. I couldn't let Morgan lose her job, especially after what I had done to get her into trouble in the first place.

"Don't worry about me," I said to her. "I'll be fine. Please try to find Gizmo."

"You won't be fine!" she yelled. "All they'll need is five minutes with you and you'll be ripped to pieces!"

Is that what Musubarin wanted? To have me taken care of, just like he had planned to have Darick taken care of on the Ember Island ferry? I set my jaw and stared at him. I had to find out what was really driving him, and why he wanted Darick and me dead.

"You need to calm down," he said to Morgan. "There's no need to get hysterical."

"Hysterical?" she said. "How about I put you in one of those cages below us and then we'll see *hysterical*."

"She'll just be there for a little while. Till the paperwork is ready and the pilot's had his break. Half an hour, max. Then we'll be up and out of here."

"Half an hour?" Morgan rubbed her temple where the vein was pulsating. "Tilexon. There'll be nothing left of her."

I pictured myself then as a wet skeleton trussed to the SubT bars, and a bloody pajama shirt lying on the dark dungeon floor below. I shuddered again.

Morgan felt for her revolver, which she did in stressful situations. It was her body's way of seeking comfort and control. If she had her gun, she'd be okay. That's how the thought-loop went, anyway. I knew because I often do the same thing with my wand, which, at that moment, was keenly missed.

"It's okay, Jax," said Morgan, who had regained her

composure. "I'll take you down, and I'll wait with you till they're ready. I'll protect you."

"No," Tilexon and I said at the same time.

"What's the difference," I said. "If they kill me now, or later at the Tower? I'm still not going to pass Go and collect a hundred dollars. But Gizmo still has a chance."

Morgan was an animal person. She especially loved her miniature pinscher called, creatively—or ironically? —Pincher.

"If you think I'm going to prioritize a polecat's life over that of my best freelance detective, you're crazy," she said. "There's no way I'm letting you die today. Or any day."

"IT'S NOT UP TO YOU," sneered Musubarin. He pulled me along again, and the handcuffs snagged my wrists, which were red with welts. Morgan ran out of the charge office and toward the stairway door that led to the subterranean cells. Tilexon dragged me along, following her.

The stairway door had been recently cut open with an axle-grinder, which probably had something to do with the fact that I had welded it closed a few days before. The door and its frame had the burn marks to prove it. Morgan stood there, feet firmly planted, ready to fight.

"You let me escort her down, or she's not going," she said.

"You know what your problem is?" Tilexon asked. "You think you're still in control. But I'm going to let you in on a little secret."

"Sod off, Musubarin," she said. "I've had enough of your stupid posturing and your arrogance. Your misguided sense of justice. You can go to hell."

"Linton!" he shouted. "Vilakazi!"

Two officers jogged up.

"I'd like you to escort Morgan out of the building."

The pair looked confused. I could practically hear the gears in their brains working. It was a heavy crunching sound, like a goblin eating over-salted popcorn.

"Escort ... Morgan?" the shorter one said. "But she's our—"

"She's not your anything," said Musubarin, eyes burning. "She's nothing. She's finished. Get her out of here."

I looked at Morgan, and I thought I saw something in her face change. It was as if a bitter breeze had reared up and snuffed out a candle.

"*Bastardis*," I hissed.

It felt as if my skin was burning where his hand touched my arm, and I would have liked nothing more than to sling a lightning spell at him and incinerate him right there in the Scorpion HQ. The magic coursed through me again, stronger this time, as if it wanted to make up for not being used earlier.

"Take your hands off me," Morgan said to the officers who were trying to subdue her. "Don't touch me!"

"You can hand in your badge on your way out," shouted Musubarin over the din of her struggling and swearing. More officers came up to us, ready to assist Linton and Vilakazi.

"You cowards," she shouted at them. "Following his orders when you know he's a fraud."

A couple of them looked ashamed for a moment, but they remained in Tilexon's corner. They knew which side of their bread was buttered; they had families to feed.

I was enraged by how quick their betrayal was, how easy. The sparks began to burn.

"Take your hands off her," I whispered. Then, louder, "Take your hands off her!"

And then I could no longer control my emotions and they came spilling out of me. First in a soft halo of magic which wobbled around me, then with a mind of its own. A jet of fire blasted out of my bound wrists, burning the metal, and my skin, as it did so. It did, however, melt the cuffs enough for me to be able to wrench them apart and snap the connecting chain. In theory, I hadn't meant to hurt Musubarin, but my instinct wasn't a fan of theory. My magic blasted him in the face, setting his hair alight and singing his eyebrows before he had pulled himself together enough to boomerang the spell back at me. The wall of heat hit me like a firenado, and if it wasn't for my coat I think I might have spontaneously combusted, and not in a good way.

The next thing I knew, Moose was screaming, and I was surrounded by officers. They were intent on marching me down to the SubT cells, while the others hauled Morgan away.

"No," I said, fighting them off. "No. I'm not going down there," but my strength was no match for theirs, and soon the metal door lurched open and we left the prefab walls and tube lights of the offices, and I was being dragged and pushed down the slippery black steps.

CHAPTER 5
FEVERISH WITH FEAR

How quickly good men can turn evil, I thought, as the officers dragged me down the craggy steps toward the SubT cells. Most of the men knew me, knew my track record. Knew that deep down, I was a good wizard who had never failed them on a case. But because a madman was in charge, they forgot their moral compasses and blindly followed orders. I was disappointed in them, but not surprised. I stopped fighting and let them take me, feeling faint as they lifted me in the air, and feverish with fear.

The stench down in the dungeon was retch-worthy. It was up my nose and in my mouth before I had time to cover my face. Feces, urine, body odor, vomit, and some other revolting smells that I didn't want to even try to identify. I swallowed the acidic bile that rose in my throat.

A few days before, the cells had been empty apart from Darick and the gray-skinned goblin. But now each of the ten cells were cramped and crowded, with men's arms waving through the bars. There was a cacophony of terse talking. I could hear sighing and moaning, too, and someone in one of the corners was weeping. The officers marched me past the flailing arms that tried to grab onto me, tried to grip my flesh, and my skin crawled. Musubarin walked behind them, a smirk of deep satisfaction on his punch-worthy face. I slipped on something slimy on the floor, and almost fell, but the officers hardened their grip on me, pulling me up, and my boots found traction again.

"Put her in cell 2A," ordered the captain, and the man clutching my arm paused and looked at his superior, frowning.

"Are you sure?" he asked. "Cell nine has the most space, and there are other women in—"

"Cell 2A, sergeant," hissed Musubarin. "Ms. Knight has an old friend in there."

The man hesitated. Blindly following orders from a mad wizard was one thing, but there was clearly something in that cell that gave him pause.

"What is it?" I asked, and he looked at me and shook his head, then looked away. One of the other officers started shouting at the inmates of my chosen cell, banging his baton on the bars and telling them to move back. Another pair of officers stood with their Tasers at the ready. Once the creatures moved away from the door, he unlocked it, and it creaked open. I saw what looked like blood on the floor, and I was sure it was splattered on the dungeon wall, too. It was too dark to see it properly, but I could smell it in the fetid air.

My heart was beating so loudly I felt deaf to the sounds in the dungeon. Anxiety snowed over my vision. There were injured orcs with shaved heads and Hammerskin tattoos, werewolves, fae. A man with a snake's head and beady eyes, and disturbing holes where his ears should have been. A huge hairy beast stood in the corner, silent, watching me with amber eyes. I couldn't see who the blood was coming from, but the trail led to the back corner. As the creatures moved backwards per the officer's directions, the filthy stone floor opened up and revealed the creature sitting on the bench at the back of the cell. It was Hux Kruq, the gray goblin. He looked up at me and smiled, and my knees almost gave way. His needle-teeth were jagged and stained; his skin reminded me of a dying slug. His black tongue shot out, licking his rubbery lips, and his eyes were evil and hungry. He stretched out his arm in my direction and gestured for me to come to him, his sharp nails cruddy with just-dried blood. His other hand disappeared into his pants. I looked away.

The officer holding my arm looked as pale as I felt. My whole body was tingling with adrenaline.

"Please," I said to him. "Please don't lock me in here."

The officer blinked at me. His upper lip was shining with sweat. The monster in the cage grunted.

"You know what he'll do to me," I said.

I wasn't in the habit of begging for my life, but desperate times call for desperate measures. I wasn't even in the cell yet but my body felt as if it was in shock. I needed my wand. I needed my crossbow and the Dragon's Eye amulet. I needed magic.

Usually fear augments my power, but the vision of Kruq there in the corner, waiting for me, did something to me. It shifted something inside me and I felt off-balance. My body was in shock, so I felt disconnected from it, and I couldn't sling spells from a body that wasn't taking orders.

The officer's Adam's apple bobbed as he swallowed.

"What are you waiting for?" yelled Musubarin. His singed hair was black at the edges, and his skin looked hot. "Hurry up and get her in there before the others get ideas about escaping."

I had to think, but my brain was a haze of panic. I needed to appeal to the man giving orders, not the ones taking them. I looked at Musubarin, forcing myself to come up with something.

"Musubarin," I said.

"Yes, Knight?" he said, irritated. "Any last words?"

Then I realized that I had been playing the wrong cards all along. I had been appealing to Musubarin's sense of right and wrong, to his sense of justice and duty. But he wasn't that kind of man. I should have been appealing to something altogether different. His ambition.

"I have something you want," I said. "I want to make a deal."

CHAPTER 6
GOBLIN LOVE GONE WRONG

I didn't have a choice. I was in my pajamas, unarmed, and about to be fed to a vicious goblin. Musubarin had my wand, my crossbow, and my magical items. Most importantly, he held Gizmo's life in his hands. I prepared myself to make a deal with the devil.

"Nothing you have will change my mind about you getting locked away in this cell," he said.

"Are you sure about that?"

Musubarin stared at me. He didn't trust me. I didn't blame him. To be fair, I had kicked him in the balls before, plus I had broken his nose with the heel of my boot. He was right to be cautious of a wily girl wizard.

"I'm going to reach into my pocket," I said.

The officers around me grabbed at their guns, ready to fire. This excited the creatures in the cages and they started shouting and grabbing again.

"Shut up!" shouted Musubarin at the inmates. "Shut up!" Then, at his team: "Will you shut them up?"

The officers got busy banging on the metal bars again, telling the prisoners to be quiet. The officer at my elbow closed and locked the cell door, and I saw the goblin's face contract in fury. Relief rushed through me; it was temporary, but welcome.

I reached into my infinity pocket and pulled out Zeel's courier delivery notebook.

"That?" sneered Musubarin. "That shabby thing? You think you'll buy your way out of here with a *book?*"

Some people don't understand the value of books. It's an easy way to judge character. In life, there's the A team and the B team. Musubarin was clearly on the B team.

"It's not just a book," I said.

It's never just *a book.*

"There are hundreds of names in here," I said. "Names, surnames, dates, addresses, telephone numbers. It's a list of all the people who have been ordering Council-banned substances from the vendors at EverShade."

Tilexon couldn't hide his interest, even though he still narrowed his eyes at me. "How did you get it?"

"None of your business," I said. I was hardly going to admit to the captain of the Scorpions that I had pickpocketed it using my quick and dirty feral magic when I was at the illegal market.

"Give it to me," he said.

"No. Not until we've decided on the terms of the deal."

"How do I know it's the real thing?" he asked.

"I don't know," I shrugged. "You're supposed to be a wizard. Don't you have a way of testing these things?"

"Gordhan," he said, and the officer holding my arm flinched. "Check the book."

I handed it to him, and he paged though it. His eyebrows shot up, and he rubbed his lips. "Looks legit," he said. Then he whistled. "You're going to want to see this, Captain. There're some crackers in here."

Musubarin crossed his arms. "I decide on the terms of the deal," he said.

"No," I said, taking the notebook back from Gordhan.

"I decide on the terms of the deal," he said again, "and you get to not be shredded by a cage of animals."

"No," I said again. I could see the desire in his eyes for my sweet piece of leverage. It was worth more to him than just sparing my life. I needed more from the deal. "I want my things back," I said. "All the things you took from me when you arrested me. Including Gizmo."

He shook his head. "Can't do. Not the ferret part, anyway. You can have your junk back but the animal handler arrived ten minutes ago. It only takes a couple of seconds to administer the shot."

My insides shriveled. I tried to hide my heartache, but tears sprang to my eyes. I swiped them away. "No ferret, no deal," I said, putting the notebook back in my pocket. Let them lock me away. The creatures in the cell could shred the book along with my body and my broken heart.

Musubarin pursed his lips and unclipped his phone from his belt. He jabbed at it, speed-dialing a number.

"Evidence room," he said, then waited to be put through.

"Put it on speaker phone," I said.

He crimped his lips harder and did as I said. Tinny elevator music blared from the speaker; a goblin ballad about love gone wrong. Then there was the sound of the call being picked up.

"Forensics," said a nasal female voice.

"Musubarin here. Has the animal handler come and gone?"

"Yes," said the voice. "Affirmative. He just left."

No! I thought, fighting the urge to weep. *No, no, no.* I felt like lying down on the rocky floor there and dissolving into nothing.

"Did he administer the injection to the ferret?" Musubarin demanded. "Yes or no?"

"Yes?" she said.

"You're uncertain?"

"He gave an injection. It's just that—"

"Get to the point. Did he administer the pento?" Agitated, Musubarin ran his hands through his burnt hair. "Did he put the animal down or not?"

"Er, no. He didn't administer the pentobarbital."

"What?"

What? What?

"I was planning on telling you, of course, Captain. But it's my son's birthday this weekend. He's turning five. The handler and I agreed that the ferret was so sweet. I said I'd adopt him. My son will adore him. The handler topped up his vaccinations—that was the injection—and then he gave me papers and everything. Said he wouldn't charge us for the call-out."

"Bring the ferret to my office," he said, looking into my eyes.

"But—"

"Immediately. The owner wants him back."

CHAPTER 7
THE VOLT CUFF

It was such a relief to be out of the subterranean cells and up in Musubarin's office. I drank in the clean air, white light, and the distinct lack of needle-toothed monsters ready to pounce. Gordhan removed my handcuffs before he disappeared to fetch Gizmo. Still, I couldn't let my guard down. Tilexon smashed a clear plastic bag down on his desk. It had my personal belongings in it. Gordhan arrived a couple minutes later with the animal carrier. Before Musubarin could stop him, he snapped open the little gate and Gizmo flew out of it and into my arms, and then shot straight into my pocket where no one could reach him but me. I stroked him through the graphene material of my coat. My heartache dissipated, but I was still trembling. Covering my mouth with my hand, I whispered a quick spell into my pocket, then reached for the bag. Musubarin stopped me.

"There is one thing," he said. "And it's a deal-maker or -breaker."

"What is it?"

He sat down at his desk and picked up a smooth black bracelet. It looked like an expensive FitBit.

"You're still under arrest," he said. "You're guilty, and I'm not dropping the charges."

"But—"

"But there's no space for you in our holding cells," he said, "And wouldn't you know it? The helicopter pilot came down with something. A stomach bug?"

"Did he eat at the canteen here?" I asked. "Because that would explain it."

"He's too ill to fly us to the Tower."

"How unfortunate," I said.

"In these situations, we put our prisoners under house arrest."

"That seems fair," I said.

"You'll have to wear this ankle cuff. I had it especially designed for prisoners like you. It's one of my favorite designs by our resident weapons engineer." Musubarin turned the sleek thing in his hands, admiring it. "It's a high-tech tracking device that will ensure you don't go anywhere you're not supposed to."

"And if I do?" I asked. "If I do go somewhere I'm not supposed to?"

He smiled. "It'll shoot a hundred thousand volts through your body."

"Harsh," I said.

He smiled a tight smile. "I just love technology, don't you? We actually nicknamed it the Volt Cuff."

"Nice to know you can kill someone anywhere in the Realm from the comfort of your own office."

"Funny," he said. "That's exactly what I said."

I wasn't too worried about the monitoring anklet. All I needed was my wand and some privacy and I'd *rumpis* the thing off my ankle. It would hurt, but not as much as eleven thousand volts would, or the knowledge that Tilexon would know my every move.

"And you'll let me walk out of here?" I asked.

"Yep," he said. "Wizard's honor."

I hated how he said that; hated that he called himself a wizard. I felt like it tarnished the name of our kin.

"Okay," I said. "It's a deal."

. . .

TILEXON PERSONALLY FITTED THE CUFF, clicking it gently into place over my ankle. As it locked, a line of five tiny green lights flicked on. I grabbed my bag of things and slung them over my shoulder, then handed the notebook over to him. He grabbed it and was poring over the pages before I left his office.

"Oh, one more thing," he said as I stepped out the door. "I forgot to mention. About the cuff."

I was in a hurry to leave, but I spun around. "Yes?"

"It can only be unlocked by a decoding chip." He tapped at his gold badge. "I made sure it would be absolutely impossible to remove otherwise. Kind of like a high-tech enchantment spell?"

I stared at him. It was bad news, but at least I was getting out there with all my limbs. It could have been far, far worse.

"Oh," he said again.

My heart sank. "Let me guess," I said. "You've just remembered something else."

He smiled at me. It was a wide, arrogant grin, and made me want to plow my fist into his face with all the strength I had left in my body.

"What?" I said, although I wasn't sure I actually wanted to know.

"The cuff also has a force field," he said. "It acts like ... what do you call that green crystal in Superman?"

I breathed in deeply and used all the willpower I had to stop from delivering that punch. Instead I balled my hands into fists.

"Kryptonite," I muttered.

"What?"

"Kryptonite," I said through my clenched teeth.

I guessed the horrible truth before he confirmed it. Despite the anger flowing through my body, there were no sparks of magic under my skin. There was no burn, no tingle. My magic was gone.

"That's it," he said. "Kryptonite. So the way this cuff works is that it sends up a force field around the prisoner, right? And this field cuts the prisoner off from the Void. So they can't access their magic, and can't cause more trouble."

He crumpled up a piece of paper on his desk and lobbed it into the corner. It was a perfect shot, and landed in the center of the bin. Then he laced his fingers behind his head and sat back in his chair, puffing out a long sigh of victory.

I looked down at the cuff, then at Musubarin again, my insides gray with dread.

"You don't know what you've done," I said.

CHAPTER 8
HIGH, OR HYPNOTIZED

The captain laughed and put his feet up on his desk, notebook in hand. I had to move fast, because if my magic was cut off, the notebook would soon disappear in his hands.

It was a conjured replica, of course, which I had swapped out at the last minute. I would never have given him the real thing, which was safe, along with Gizmo, in my pocket. Who knows what someone like Musubarin would do with a book like that?

I started jogging, then sprinting, and as I escaped out the back door on the ground level, I heard Musubarin's voice yelling from two floors above.

"Wiza-a-ard!"

I was in a bad place, cut off from my magic, but I couldn't help smiling. In difficult times you have to celebrate the small victories. I had just negotiated my way out of a painful death with nothing but fresh air and a little whispered conjuring spell. Honestly, I hadn't thought he'd fall for it. A wizard should know the difference between a magically cloned copy and the real thing, right?

But I was beginning to realize that Tilexon's magical intelligence was on par with that of a glazed donut. His magic had no depth to it. If there was such thing as magical EQ, his registered low on the scale. My theory was that he was this way because he had so little empathy. You can't forge powerful magic without empathy, not on your own, anyway. Not without the help of magical items.

A glance down to my volt cuff quickly wiped the smug off my face. At least he still had access to his magic. I had nothing. And, speaking of magical items, I had those elemental fragments to find.

Of course, he'd come after me. He had my GPS coordinates in real time and a grudge the size of Alaska. I would only be able to outrun him for so long. I needed a strategy.

I FELT Gizmo moving in my pocket, and I took him out for a quick hug.

"Thought I'd lost you," I mumbled into his fur. Which, I'll admit, is an ironic thing to say to a ferret whose magical ability is to find things.

"I need you to point me in the direction of those fragments," I said, but he just leaned into me for another hug. We didn't even know what they were, so it was kind of like a ferrety version of *Mission: Impossible*. He kept leaning into me, and it made me wonder if he knew how close he had come to dying. Thank the Void for that woman in the evidence room who saved his life. When this whole mess was over I'd send her a fruit basket, *a la* Sugar Shagar. The thought of those muffins made the werewolf in my stomach wake up with a yawn. It was a special kind of torture knowing there was a hamper of food waiting for us at home, but no time, and no way to get there. I emptied my Scorpion-branded personal belongings bag and looked at the summoning ring Ferra had engineered for me. I tried to summon my motorbike, on the off-chance it would still work, but the spell fell flat. Still, I put the ring on, as well as my two necklaces. I moved to clip my mother's silver wand to my utility belt, but then remembered I was wearing pajamas. I clipped the crossbow to my back. I wouldn't be able to sling spells with it, but the arrows would still work. I put on my charm bracelet last, and looked at the djinn stone and the spent bullet Darick have given me. I wondered where he was. Gizmo leapt back into my pocket, and I began to walk again. I didn't know where I was going, but it felt good to move.

IT WAS difficult to see the state of the city: piled high with burning garbage, storefronts smashed. The Johannesburg sky, which is usually a clear blue canvas, looked dull and ashy. It made me think of the destruction of *The Copper Cog and Ale,* and I had to blink the tears away.

Seeing Johannesburg like that was devastating, so to mitigate the hopelessness welling up inside me, I thought of the people and creatures I loved. It was the only thing I could do to motivate myself to keep going, and to find the fragments. If not for the people I loved, why else was I trying to save the Realm? So that Ferra and her family could escape the fox den and rebuild their house. So that I could find Nilve SaltySnap. So that Bron would find me again, and we would work out a way to return him to his human shifter form. So that Morgan could pick up the pieces of her life, and Darick and I could tentatively begin some kind of future together.

I walked and walked. Over crackling glass shards, over tarmac stained with vomit and oil and greasy orc blood. The traffic lights no longer worked, but it didn't matter much, because there were hardly any cars left on the roads.

The people I walked past made me shudder. They all had that same blank expression as I'd seen on the woman in the floral dress who had walked into the Scorpion SUV earlier. It was as if they were all high, or hypnotized. They had bruises on their bodies, like they were just walking into things and not noticing the pain. I didn't want to admit it, but they were like indifferent zombies. Zombies that didn't want to eat your brain—again, let's celebrate the small victories—but zombies nonetheless. There was nothing behind those masks they were wearing for faces, no spark of intelligence or emotion. It was like they were being controlled by some faraway force, a toddler with a remote control. I couldn't figure out what was wrong with the untouched people, but I didn't have time to work it out. They didn't seem to be a threat. I wouldn't know where to start, anyway, if I were to try to help them. Was it some kind of magical disease? Perhaps I'd go to *Mason & Sons* for their opinion.

Then it struck me. *Mason & Sons*. The ancient magical apothecary. So, the volt cuff was cutting off my personal magic, but that didn't mean I couldn't use other people's manufactured magic. I had experienced it myself when I had been locked in Slyden Abarim's enchanted basement: my own magic had been cut off, but the magical potion —*Nebulam*—that I had bought from the apothecary still worked beautifully. All I needed to do was to head to the old apothecary and load up on as many useful potions as I could get my hands on. It wouldn't be the same as having my own magic, but at least I'd—literally—have some tricks up my sleeve. Armed with a plan of action, I immediately felt better. I began walking a little faster, and within half an hour I approached the square where the *Mason & Sons* building had stood for over a century.

What I saw made my skeleton freeze. Had I taken a wrong turn somewhere? Had the proprietors forged some special

brand of magic and made their building relocate, or disappear? Because gone was the solid facade with the handsome gold lettering on the wall. Gone was the security
dwarf who usually guarded the front door with a
vengeance. Gone were the groaning shelves of every
potion and tincture and glamour you could think of. As I
got nearer, I saw that the building had not been magically
moved or made invisible, but it had been razed. *Mason &
Sons* had been burnt to the ground.

CHAPTER 9
CRACKED

Broken medicine bottles lay smashed on the ground, metal tins scorched and melted. The antique newspapered wall that I had admired on my first visit lay crumbled at my feet. Old black bricks were still warm to the touch. I walked over them, crushing cinders as I walked, and the sour smoke I saw swirling around me was also in my chest; a whirlwind of grainy, bitter sadness. Not a vial or a spell book remained. Decades of work, wizardry, and wisdom lay in ashes.

The smoke stung my eyes. That was my excuse, anyway, as seemingly endless tears flowed down my cheeks. I sat down on a warm block that may have once been the counter, and I couldn't help weeping. Whether I admitted it or not, Musubarin had given me the fright of my life, and my body was still reeling from the shock of the trauma down at the SubT cells. I thought I had lost Gizmo, which had speared me in the heart, and, despite his comforting shape in my pocket, I still had not recovered. I felt naked, literally and figuratively, stripped of my regular clothes and my magic. My worry for Ferra nagged at me, and I felt utterly alone. I cried and cried until my body felt weak.

Slowly, the sorrow transformed into a slow-burning fury. Who the *faex* did these skinhead orcs think they were? They had razed all the institutions that were sacred to not only me, but the whole wizarding community. *If Raguk Magra were here*, I thought to myself, my anger flaring in my chest, *if that bloody Hammerskin were here, I'd drive a hot metal poker through his heart, and I would enjoy doing it.*

"Hello?" said a voice, making me catapult off the mound I was sitting on. "Hello?" he said again. I looked up and saw a stooped figure dressed in a scorched wizard robe. His face was blackened with soot, and one of the lenses of his gold-framed spectacles was cracked. It was old man Mason.

"Hello," I said, wiping the tears away from my face. My hand came away gray.

Under his left eye there was a pouch of purple blood, and I saw that his right hand was charred. I flinched when I saw it, thinking of how painful it must be.

"You tried to defend yourself," I said, looking at his hand.

He looked down, as if he had forgotten about his burnt skin, and then nodded. "Tried, yes."

The old wizard was trembling as he leaned on his blackened staff. I was too afraid to ask what had become of his father, and his grandfather. Then I noticed a black shape on the ground with spokes and melted rubber wheels. Great-grandfather Mason's wheelchair.

"How can they do this?" I asked, speaking past the lump in my throat. "How can they be so cold-blooded?"

"Evil lurks in every heart," said the wizard.

I felt like weeping again, but I pulled myself together. Now was not the time to fold in on myself. We stood in silence for a moment, surrounded by devastation and the smell of smoke. Is this what *The Copper Cog* looked like now? And Ferra's home? And what had become of the Copperfield Institute?

I showed the old man the cuff on my ankle. "Scorpion-issue," I said. "It's cutting off my magic. Do you think you'd be able to remove it with a *rumpis* spell?"

He stooped to inspect it with his watery eyes, the crack in his the lens of his specs looking like an angry spiderweb. Then he stepped back with a sigh. "Too dangerous," he said. "It would break your ankle."

I felt chilled, imagining being unable to walk, or run. I'd take the cuff over being hobbled, at least till I had a better idea. I could try to get hold of Musubarin's chip, which was baked into the golden badge in his chest. But that option filled me with dread, too.

"I came here in the hope of buying some potions," I said. "I feel so vulnerable without my magic."

He looked at me and nodded sadly. He still had his magic, but he had lost everything else. We were both in impossible situations. He coughed, and his chest rattled like a cage of old bones.

"I'm afraid I don't have anything to offer you," he said, sweeping his hand across what used to be his famous building.

But his words gave me an idea. He didn't have any potions for me, but he was a wealth of information. He knew more about magic and the Realm than anyone else I knew.

"Mister Mason," I said. "I'm searching for the elemental fragments. Do you have any idea what they are?"

The wizard frowned at me and clacked his teeth. "Elemental fragments?" I could see from his facial expression that he suspected I was one crayon short of a box.

"Earth, air, water," I said. "Once you bring them together you get a fire, a black magic blaze that can destroy the Realm."

The man blinked at me. "I'm not certain I've heard that before."

My shoulders dropped. The old man pushed his spectacles up the bridge of his nose. "That isn't to say they don't exist. There are many magical items that are kept secret for the safety of the Realm."

"I need to know what the fragments are, so that I can find them and make sure they don't fall into the wrong hands. The Silvano Clan already has the HighFire Crown, and their power is proliferating every day. If they get hold of the other two fragments..."

There was no need to finish the sentence.

"I need to know what they are," I said again, mostly to myself, then looked at the old man again. "It's all in a book. A book I was urged to read."

I left out the part about my housekeeping specter slamming that particular book onto the floor over and over till I eventually got the message to pick it up and read it. He fiddled with the bent gold frames again and peered at me.

"A book?" he said, perking up.

"It's about vampire lore, written centuries ago by a man named Griffin Zolastaro."

Of course, old man Mason was so ancient he may have actually been alive when the book was written. He was probably celebrating his fortieth birthday party with cake and ale while Zolastaro was sprouting milk teeth.

"Zolastaro?" muttered the old wizard. "Zolastaro." He rolled the name around in his mouth and frowned.

"You know of him?" I asked.

"No," he said. "I'm sorry I can't help you."

I felt defeated, then, and the small amount of hope I had drained away.

The wizard cleared his throat of tumbleweeds. "But I think I know who can."

CHAPTER 10

GRAY WITH ASH

"Ms. Knight," old man Mason said, leaning on his blackened staff. "Have you ever had the pleasure of meeting a Madame Woolf?"

It took me a second to register the name, because it felt so out of place there in the bleak wasteland of what used to be *Mason & Sons*. Scarlet-lipped Madame Woolf was the proprietor of The Jupiter Drawing Room, the most luxurious and upmarket bordello in Johannesburg. She had recently hired me for a job. Her place of business was being frequented by a particularly reckless vampire, which, as you can imagine, had not been good for business. A customer of hers—a man in pink boxer shorts—had died on my watch, and the vicious creature who had murdered him escaped out the window. It wasn't a career highlight, that's for sure, but I did get vengeance in the end, and another notch on my bedpost.

"Madame Woolf?" I said, "Of the Jupiter Drawing Room?"

"Correct!" he said, a little too enthusiastically, and we were both punished by another bout of his hacking into his elbow. When he had recovered, he continued in a hoarse voice. "Woolf is an expert on history. She is committed to the subject and studies it doggedly. If there is anyone in the city who knows about that Zolastaro chap, it will be her."

I felt like hugging the old wizard, so I did. He was surprised, flinching at first, but then his body relaxed and he returned the embrace.

"Thank you," I said.

I LEFT HIM THERE, and he continued to shuffle through the remains of the magical apothecary, muttering to himself as he did so. I looked back to check on him one last time, and as I took my eyes off the ground in front of me I tripped and fell, hard, on a hundred shattered bottles and vials, lacerating my exposed knees and shins. It felt as if I had been stung by a dozen hornets.

I swore under my breath, then began to pick the shards of smoky glass of all shapes and shades out of my skin. Ruby rivulets ran down my shins. Swearing again, I looked at what I had tripped over. It was the stuffed crocodile, the one that used to hang over the counter at *Mason & Sons,* its mouth shaped artfully into a grin. There was no smile now. His body was eaten away by fire. He looked like an abstract sculpture in charcoal.

With the last of the glass extricated from my shredded skin, I took a calming breath. I was about to stand up when a small green vial caught my eye. It was as scorched as the other merchandise, but there still seemed to be some liquid in the bottle. I picked it up. It was still warm, and the black of the exterior came off on my palms. The cork had been damaged by the fire, and most of the potion had leaked out, but there was still a splash left over. I studied the label, which was ink on ebony. I had to tilt it away to make out what it said.

SUMMONING POTION.

I wasn't sure what I would do with it, but I had a feeling it would come in handy, so I adjusted the cork as much as I could to stop further loss, and slipped it into my pocket.

I WAS TEMPTED to use the new potion on summoning my bike, which I missed. But I had a feeling I'd need it for something more important, so I decided to walk to The Jupiter Drawing Room. It only took me twenty minutes, and I needed the exercise to shake some endorphins into my blood and to keep my mind from unspooling from the anxiety I felt tingling all over.

I also worried that when I got there, the famous bordello would be in a similar state to *Mason & Sons*, but I needn't have worried. The Victorian-era style house was standing as proudly as ever, and the antique-looking roses in the front garden bloomed bright cerise despite the smoke and violence in the air.

I knocked on the ornate front door, and looked down at the vintage bronze doorknob. I had destroyed a couple of those, along with the doors they belonged to, the last time I had been there. I hoped that Woolf didn't hold it against me.

A woman in a red satin corset opened the door and looked down her nose at me. I didn't blame her. I was still wearing my *Rocking the Realm* T-shirt and sleep-shorts, and my skin was gray with ash.

"We're not hiring," she said, and tried to close the door. I wedged my boot in so that she couldn't.

"I'm not here for a job," I said. "I need to see Madame."

"Madame is not seeing anyone today," the woman said.

I couldn't help but to admire her costume. It was beautiful, and very flattering. I had liked the look of it on myself, too, when I was here on that job, but it had proven to be too restrictive for me and I had ended up ripping it off and dropping it on the steel spiral staircase.

I took a step forward. I wanted to get in and lock the door before I was spotted by some skinhead orcs, who seemed to now lurk on every corner.

"She'll want to see me," I said.

The woman crossed her arms, and the emerald on her necklace caught the light and flashed at me. "I doubt it," she said.

"Tell her it's Jacquelyn Denna Knight."

She stared at me for a moment longer, and then seemed to decide I was not the enemy. She stuck her head out the doorway and looked left and right. "You'd better come in," she muttered, pulling me inside. "It's not safe out there."

CHAPTER 11

NO ORDINARY KNOCKING SHOP

"Ms. Knight," said the scarlet-lipped brothel-keeper. "I've been expecting you."

Madame Woolf sat behind her elegant ball-and-claw desk. Her chair was stately, and the backdrop of rich velvet curtains made me feel as if I were having an audience with a queen ... if queens were in the habit of running houses of ill repute.

But this was no ordinary knocking shop. Woolf had curated the interior design over decades, creating the most elegant, luxurious brothel in the city. I didn't know why it was still standing, but I'm glad it was. I'd be sorry to see the beautiful furniture burn, the brocade turn black. I realized then how fleeting everything was. How the things I thought would stand forever were just a flame and a gust away from being demolished. My thoughts were running away with me, but Woolf reined them in with her voice, which she knew how to leverage for maximum effect. Her accent was crisp, her speech eloquent, and it made me wonder about her life, and the events that had put her in that room with me that day.

"You've been expecting me?" I said, hoping she wasn't planning on asking me to pay for the damage I had caused on my mission when I was last there. A destroyed period costume; a few doors; a couple of scorch marks on the elegant vanilla and velvet wallpaper.

She soundlessly slid open a drawer and retrieved a thick cream envelope with my name on it, then extended it to me. I stepped forward and took it. Just what I needed. More bills.

"I trust you'll find it satisfactory," she said, and her lips curled into a hint of a smile. "You'll find that I added a bonus for your excellent work."

I opened the expensive-looking envelope and peered inside. A fat bundle of two hundred rand notes were tied together with a thin silver thread.

"Thank you," I said. "I wasn't expecting this."

Of course, Woolf wouldn't have known that I had choked just as I was about to deliver my *coup de grace* to the vampire who had been picking off her customers. She wouldn't know that the bloodsucker had escaped out the window because I had ashed the creature the very next night. It had taken longer than I expected, but I had removed the immediate threat, which meant that Madame Woolf's customers were relatively safe. For now.

"It's very generous of you," I said.

Woolf shrugged. "Business has been excellent."

Most shops in the city were closed or destroyed, so she was lucky. "It's the nature of the business," said Woolf. "In difficult times, people need to be able to escape. And where better," she asked gesturing at the grand room, "than here? Some of the customers don't even ask for a room. They just want to be here. It's another world, different from the difficult one outside of these doors."

"Madame Woolf," I said. "You don't need me to tell you that you've done an excellent job in recreating a Victorian-era ... experience," I said. "Old man Mason said you're an expert on history."

"Oh," she said, with a gentle laugh. "I don't know about that. I'm hardly an *expert*."

"But you know a great deal about the history of the city?" I said. "And its people?"

"I do," she said. "I find it fascinating. But I must admit, my tastes do run to the dark side."

"What do you mean?"

"I have no interest in the history of the gold mines, or the various period architecture in the city center. What fascinates me is the people. Especially the eccentric people who lived here before us."

"You're the exact person I need to speak to, then," I said. "I need to know about an author who lived here in the eighteen hundreds."

"An author?" she said. "That shouldn't be difficult. There weren't many around in those days."

Hope swirled in my chest.

"Zolastaro," I said. "Griffin Zolastaro."

Woolf narrowed her eyes at me, thinking. "Zolastaro?" she said. "It sounds like the name of an arcade time machine."

"Yes," I said. The stage name of a hack magician. An arcade time machine. A gold mining magnate. A turncoat. A vampire aficionado. The author of the book that is going to save the Realm.

"I HAVE OIL PAINTINGS," Woolf said, and I smiled politely. I wasn't interested in an art show. I needed to get the information on Zolastaro and get out of there, no matter how luxurious it felt to be in a room away from murdered Khargols and zombies and smoking trash-lined streets.

"A rather valuable collection," she said. "I keep them hidden from my customers and staff. Certain pleasures must be reserved for oneself alone, don't you agree?"

Yep, I thought. *Yep, yep, yep. Can we just get on with it?*

I didn't want to be rude, but there were magical items at large, and, unlike hippies at a mountain retreat, they were not going to find themselves.

"Paintings?" I said.

"Portraits, specifically," she said. "I never let anyone see them. But I'll make an exception for you."

"Thank you," I said. I sure as hell hoped this would lead somewhere. I could practically hear the clock of doom ticking in my head.

She stood up and strode toward the massive bookshelf. "You enjoy books, Ms. Knight," she said. "Come and stand here next to me, and choose a book."

I walked over. With as many books as this, Woolf was certainly on the A team. I reached out for a yellow spine, and Woolf said, "Not that one."

I frowned and went for a burgundy one, but before I touched it, she said, "Not that one, either."

I looked more carefully, and then I saw it. A fat black spine with silver lettering: magical symbols I could not decipher. I touched it, and Woolf smiled. Then I pulled it out, and she grabbed my arm and looked me in the eye. Hers were twinkling. There was a deep clunking sound, and the polished wooden floor we were standing on began to move, and the bookshelf swung one hundred and eighty degrees, depositing us in the secret chamber next door.

CHAPTER 12

PORTRAITS DON'T TALK

The secret chamber smelled like a museum. It was crowded with artifacts, and there was hardly room to move. There were framed paintings on the walls and leaning towers of books. Tables groaned under the weight of jewelry, silver antiques, and more books.

"Wow," I said, and Woolf's face shone. She picked up the object closest to her, a playful pewter bell on an ivory ring. "This is a Victorian teething ring," she said. "Isn't it dear?"

Then she showed me a vintage wig and some rubber underwear. "Imagine wearing these," she said.

"About the portraits," I said.

"Of course. This way."

Together we scanned all the paintings on the wall, but Zolastaro was not there. I was annoyed. This had been a particularly time-consuming dead-end.

"Oh, don't fret, dear," she said. "I don't have space on the wall for all the art I have."

She led me to the corner, where a metal cabinet stood. It was battered and dusty.

"I don't let the housekeepers in here," she said, blowing dust off the handle before touching it. With a tug she pulled the drawer out. It was one of those long, deep spaces which could house a hundred different kitsch posters in a tourist store. This particular chamber, however, carried more canvases than the Louvre.

"Holy..." I said.

"It's a comprehensive collection," said Woolf. "If Zolastaro was an author, his portrait will be here. No one famous escaped without a portrait in those days."

That was the good news. The bad news was that it would take me at least a decade to wade through every painting to work out who was who.

"I don't suppose it's in alphabetical order," I joked, and Woolf smiled.

"Honestly," she said. "Despite years of research, I don't know who half of them are."

A buzzing sound reached us from Madame Woolf's office, so with a pat on my shoulder for luck and stamina, she left me to my new art appreciation course. I sighed and started paging through the old canvases.

Some of the paintings were expertly executed, and made me want to stop and admire them, despite my desire to get going. Others were clumsy, rushed, with no artistic flair, and were easy to page past. I felt Gizmo move around in my pocket, and then his head appeared.

"Hello, minion," I said. "I need your whiskers on this job."

He nodded and looked at the stack of canvases. I wasn't sure how it would work. I imagined setting him up at a table with the art spread out in front of him. He'd be wearing bifocals and tiny white cotton gloves. But it turned out that he didn't need any of that. He just stuck out his snowy paw and selected a painting, as if we were playing tricks with a deck of cards.

I opened the bundle of canvases where he had indicated, and a man with jet black hair stared back at me. The portrait was so lifelike it gave me goosebumps. At the bottom of the painting, in a tiny, neat handwriting, it said *Griffin Zolastaro*.

Thank the Void for small mercies. And for magical pet ferrets.

"Mister Zolastaro," I said. "I am pleased to make your acquaintance."

Gizmo glanced up at me, perhaps thinking I'd finally lost my marbles—not that I had many to begin with—and angled his head.

"Well done," I whispered to him. "Thank you."

Not for the first time, I wished I had a bag of ferret treats in my pocket.

Instead I unclipped the canvas and pulled it out from the drawer, then laid it on a table nearby. On second thoughts, I decided to clip it up over one of the paintings hanging on the wall, so I could inspect it properly in its new burnished frame. I stood there, looking into Griffin Zolastaro's deep green eyes.

"Yes?" I said. "What do you have to tell me?"

Gizmo made a funny squeaking sound, like a dog's toy. A rubber cartoon-bone.

"I know, I know," I said. "You think I'm crazy. Portraits don't talk."

He squeaked again. It was probably ferret-speak for "*Get thee to* the *insane asylum, pronto.*"

I looked at him, then looked at the painting again. Zolastaro stared back at me. His eyes were deep emerald abysses. I got the feeling that he definitely wanted to tell me something.

. . .

"I'M LISTENING."

I may have imagined it then, but I think I saw Gizmo roll his eyes. That's when I remembered the potion in my pocket. It was a tablespoon, at most. Hardly enough to do any kind of magic with. Would a summoning spell even work on an old portrait? I had my doubts. Still, I needed to try it. I reached into my pocket and took out the blackened glass bottle and edged out its flame-gnawed cork. I couldn't help but feel a little bit sorry for myself. Of all the magic I had previously been capable of, I was reduced to this. I felt like the equivalent of a tuk-tuk being held together with string and a prayer.

The cork came out, and I took a suspicious sniff of the contents. Alcohol and herbs. Soap and cinnamon bark. It smelled more like Old Spice aftershave than a summoning potion, but who was I to judge it? The last potion I had made almost blew up the school laboratory at the Copper-field Institute. Turns out that I'm more talented at blowing things up than mixing things together. It's also the reason my kitchen equipment huddles together in fright when I come anywhere near them. It's not like I can blame them. Besides, they've probably been eaten by my horror plant, so even if there were bad feelings, I wouldn't talk ill of the recently devoured.

I looked down at the vial in my hands, then up at the portrait. I felt ridiculous and desperate at the same time. Before I lost my nerve, I threw the contents of the bottle at the painting and hoped for the best. I worried that the paint would start crackling and peeling away, and I'd have yet another apology to make to Madame Woolf. But what happened was worse. I watched and watched Zolastaro's face, and nothing changed.

CHAPTER 13
THE CHAOS JAR

Then, suddenly, there was a minute movement. The slightest twitch of a nose, as if he could also smell the overpowering Old Spice. Soon he blinked, and just as I was wondering if I had imagined it, he blinked again.

"Zolastaro!" I yelled, giving Gizmo a fright. "Griffin Zolastaro! Can you hear me?"

The man's black eyebrows wiggled, and then his jaw moved, as if he was stretching it. As if his muscles were stiff from so many decades of holding utterly still. His dark limpid eyes sparkled as they came to life.

Finally, he shook his hair out of his face and lost his dreamy look, and he focused on me.

"Oh!" he said. "Where are we? Is this heaven?"

"Hang on," I said. "I'm the one who's supposed to be asking the questions."

"You are?" he said. "Who are you?"

"Do you mean," I said, "That you've been dead for over a century and you still don't know if there is a heaven or hell?"

"Oh, I know there's a hell," he said. He smoothed his hair and I glimpsed his elegant fingers.

I would have liked to press him on that, but I knew the potion would only last a few more minutes, at most. It was already evaporating at the edges.

"I have an urgent question," I said. "About the book you wrote. *Vampire Lore*."

"Oh!" he said. "That was an interesting one to research."

"You were the vampire authority in your day?" I asked. "An academic?"

"An academic?" he said, and threw his head back, roaring with laughter. "No, no, no. Not quite."

Disappointment bloomed inside me like a black rose, rising, opening, and dying.

"But you wrote the book. It was a ... serious book, right?"

The laughter vanished. "Oh, yes. Deadly serious. But I was

no academic. An academic did not have access to the information that I was privy to."

"Where did you get it from, then?"

"I used to ... mix in ... interesting circles," he said. "I was on the fringe, myself, you see. I couldn't be my true self in society. I had to leave it for the dark rooms and the witching hours."

"What does that mean?"

"I socialized with less ... savory folk," he said.

"Vampires?"

"Vampires. Werewolves. I found their company more stimulating than the magnates and prospectors. They were all after gold. I was after something else."

"An early death," I said, and he laughed again.

"I like you," he said. "What did you say your name was?"

"I'm Jacquelyn," I said. "I'm a wizard."

He looked surprised again.

"Well," he said. "This is interesting indeed. Summoned by a wizard from the future."

At least he didn't say *girl wizard*.

"If you were friends with vampires," I said, "why did you

write that book? Why would you bother warning readers about the New Dawn?"

"My fellow outcasts and I had no ambition, no agenda. We were mountain climbers, truth-seekers. Politics was not our bag. But then we got wind of the strategy to bring on the New Dawn, and we knew we had to warn the public. I was the only one with a formal education, so I wrote it. They helped me with the details. We published a flyer at first, a pamphlet, but no one took us seriously. I decided a book would carry more gravitas, so we worked to finish that, and published it to a resounding silence. It was a hard life on the mines. The mortals were not interested in fairytales. One of the missionary men even burned a few copies. You'd think after that kind of attention I would have moved a few copies, but it fell flat, and we stopped trying, and the New Dawn never arrived."

"Not in your lifetime, anyway," I said. "But vampires appear to be patient bastards."

"What?" Griffin said, pushing his hair back. "Have they finally made a move? What year is it?"

"2019," I said. "They're making their move."

"Ha!" he said. "Vindicated, at last. Not that I care anymore, of course."

I looked at him.

"Maybe I care just a little bit," he said. "Tell me, is it Bald Ass?"

"Excuse me?"

"Bald Ass. He was by far the most ambitious little twerp of the lot."

"Do you mean Baldassare?" I asked. "Acheron?"

"That's him. A right upstart, that vampire. We should have ashed him when we had the chance, instead of writing a useless book. We believed in non-violence, then. We used to smoke a lot of weed."

"Weed?"

"What?" he said. "Do you think you lot invented marijuana?"

"No, I just—"

"Opium, too, and hard tack. There were a lot of drugs going around those days, but of course, that kind of information doesn't make it into the history books."

"I'm finding this utterly fascinating," I said. "But we don't have much time. I can see the spell fading already." Zolastaro's neck was already frozen, and I was sure his mouth would be next.

"Right," he said. "You had a question. Ask away. Anything. Happy to oblige."

"The New Dawn," I said. "The elemental fragments."

"Ah."

"You didn't name them in the book for fear that the wrong kind of person would bring the fragments together."

"Right."

"So ... I need to know what they are. So I can make sure they don't fall into the wrong hands."

"Hmm," he said, stroking his chin, which seemed to be in the process of freezing, too.

"What?"

"How do I know," he said, "That your pretty hands are not *the wrong hands?*"

"Ah," I said. "Look. Vampires killed my parents. I've been fighting vampires my whole life. I was staking vampires' hearts when other kids were chasing Pokêmons."

He looked at me for a long minute.

"Please," I said. "The potion is wearing off. Please tell me what the fragments are. My guess is that the earth element is the HighFire Crown."

"Correct," he said, nodding, but his face got stuck mid-nod.

"Please."

Griffin saw the desperation in my face, and softened. "Okay," he said. "I'll compromise."

We don't have ti-i-i-i-i-me, I was screaming inside. *No time for compromises!*

"I'll tell you what the air fragment is," he said. His chin was no longer moving, and I saw his lips begin to stiffen. "Have you ever heard of the Chaos Jar?"

"What?" I said, making sure I had heard him right. "The Chaos Jar?"

"You'll know it when you see it. It looks like blue lightning locked in a jar. It'll be sequestered somewhere safe," he said.

"Nowhere is safe anymore," I said. "That's why I need to find it."

That was one of the reasons the Silvanos were allowing the Hammerskins to tear up the Realm, wasn't it? Sowing panic, and at the same time, hoping to unearth the missing fragments.

"The Chaos Jar," I said again. "Got it. Thank you."

"I won't tell you what the third fragment is," he said, and my pulse sprinted. "That's the compromise." His lips were moving in slow motion.

"No!" I yelled. "You have to tell me! What is the third fragment?"

Water. I needed to know what the water one was. It wouldn't necessarily be water of course, just something liquid, with potent magic.

But there was nothing left of the summoning potion.

"The water fragment ... if you are who you say you are," he drawled, fighting the paralysis. "Then you already have what you need."

CHAPTER 14
FERRET RADAR

I left The Jupiter Drawing Room feeling frustrated, but at least I had a way forward. So often I feel as if I'm losing the battle, but I've also learned to trust the process. It's a bit like my domino theory. You can't let the case overwhelm you, even if you have nothing. Even if you have less than nothing. You need to trust that as you investigate, as you follow the leads—no matter how oblique they may seem—they will lead you forward. And as long as you knew you're moving forward, there was nothing to panic about. In my paranormal detective cases all I needed was the first domino. The first domino brings with it momentum and direction. In this case, it was the Chaos Jar.

A bottle of blue lightning, hidden somewhere under lock and key, or, more likely, a complicated elf enchantment, because everyone knows that elven enchantments were impossible to break. That's why the HighFire Crown was in the Pavaris mansion in the first place. And when Pavaris had become greedy and inadvertently put the Crown on the market, he had shattered over a century of status quo.

If one of the fragments was up for grabs, the vampires must have thought, then they could snag the others, too.Decades of biding their time, refining their strategy, and sharpening their fangs was about to pay off in a big way.

"The Chaos Jar," I said to Gizmo, and he nodded. It was a good sign, but I didn't get my hopes up. This wasn't my first roller derby. I knew it wouldn't be that easy. But I had a name, and a direction, and a magical albino ferret called Gizmo. I was going to grab that first domino, and see where it took me.

IT TOOK ages to walk the way Gizmo directed me. I should have felt exhausted after the day I'd had, but my body was running on adrenaline and my limbs wanted to keep moving. After a couple of hours we were out of the city and the architecture gradually transformed from towering solarscrapers to houses hiding behind eight-foot tall walls festooned with glittering silver barbed wire. I kept walking, and soon I began to recognize the environment. I had been there before. Recently. It wasn't the white picket fence and flamingos of Greenside, or the luxury mansions of the Elf Estate. It was a well-maintained but understated neighborhood, the kind I grew up in. Purple-blossomed Jacaranda trees on the sidewalks, swing sets in the gardens. And then it made sense: it was the kind of suburb wizard families would live in. And that's when I realized that we were on our way to the Belore house.

Are you sure? I wanted to ask Gizmo as we stopped outside the house I recognized. Was he getting confused? Was his ferret radar malfunctioning? But I knew that the polecat had never failed me, so I took a deep breath, pressed the doorbell, and rattled the pedestrian gate. Of course, there was no answer. Mr. and Mrs. Belore were buried at the Oaktown Cemetery; I had felt the rich red soil in my hands before I flung it onto their matching coffins. In a slightly less charming memory, I had seen Ametrix Belore's decomposing body stuffed into a cheap trunk together with a snickering plague of hungry city rats eager to speed up the job. I still had nightmares of Obsidian Hill, and I hoped I'd never have to traverse that kind of pocket realm again.

I DIDN'T HAVE A CHOICE. I needed to break into the esteemed wizards' home and search for the Jar. I readied my muscles and parkoured up the plastered wall and jumped down on the other side. It was a long way down, so I fell in a soft tumble as to not break cartilage or snap any bones. Once I was on the property, I tried the front door. It was locked. I almost slung a small fire spell to melt the lock, but then I remembered I no longer had access to the Void. A fleeting thought then, was that if I no longer had magic, was I still a wizard?

I knew I had wizard blood, but was that enough? I didn't know. And I had no one to ask.

I picked up a rock from the garden and used it to break the glass of one of the windows. It was a small one, the only one I could find without burglar bars, and I had to squeeze myself through the teeth of the glass. My trench coat protected me from the worst of the scrapes, but I still felt the shards biting into my skin.

The Belore house was in darkness, and when I flipped the switches I saw that the lights no longer worked. I suppose dead wizards don't pay their electricity bills. I didn't have my utility belt, so I didn't have my penlight. Usually in this case I'd light my wand with an *illumino* spell, but, again, I had to stop myself reaching for it. I had a rush of sympathy for untouched folk. Life without magic felt gray and shallow, and relentlessly difficult.

I followed Gizmo's snout, stumbling over things in the dark. The house was in a mess. Ferra had told me they were still trying to contact the twins' next of kin, who was their aunt in Manhattan, but so far they'd had no luck. There was also a cousin, twice removed: a wizard who lives in Dublin. Neither returned Ferra's calls.

I moved through the living room, trying not to fall over kids' toys and sofa cushions. I raced up the stairs to where I knew Ametrix and Francis's bedroom and office was. I felt guilty invading such an intimate space. I knew it was irrational; skeletons don't care about privacy. But I couldn't help the feeling of discomfort, like little hands pulling at my coat.

"The bedroom, Gizmo?" I asked. "Are you sure?"

The ferret didn't need to answer me, because something odd happened. The Dragon's Eye amulet—the one which used to belong to Ametrix—started glowing. I felt its warmth in my chest, and I looked down to see it flickering with a deep orange light. It got hotter and hotter until I had to take it off, fearing it would burn me.

We were playing hide and seek, and the amulet was telling me that I was really close to what I was looking for. I spun slowly around the room, wondering where the Chaos Jar was.

Certainly not in the open. I used the necklace like a compass, directed by the heat of its glow. It led me to the large antique mirror that hung over the bath. I was startled by my own reflection: skin still smeared by ash, eyes ablaze with purpose, palm flaming with the light of the Dragon's Eye.

CHAPTER 15

MERCURY MEMBRANE

"The mirror?" I said out loud. I moved toward it and held its scalloped edges, wondering if I needed to take it down from the wall in order to access some kind of magical safe behind it. I tried to slip my fingers underneath the glass, but it was cemented firmly to the wall. I was puzzled, and at the same time, second-guessing both myself and Gizmo.

Honestly, I thought to myself. *What are the chances of such a powerful magical item just happening to be in the house of a wizard I knew?*

Or knew of, anyway. I'd never met the man while he was alive. But my point remained. It seemed to be heavy on the coincidence. Then I remembered the first phone call I received from Eafaris Belore, when he hired me to search for his missing father. He said the last time Ametrix was seen alive was before he left for a meeting with the Council. Now, no ordinary wizard just *meets* with the Council, just like no ordinary person just meets with the president for tea. Ametrix was clearly working for the Council in some way. Perhaps he was the designated Keeper of the Chaos Jar, which explained why he was killed by the Silvanos. His body had been in terrible shape when I found it at Obsidian Hill. Had he been abducted and tortured for information by the clan? Once they realized that he wouldn't give them the location of the Jar, they had killed him.

When I had seen all the unmarked graves at the cemetery that night in the haunted forest, while standing on the soft dark soil, I had thought the selection of those wizards had been random, but now I understood that it had not been random at all. The Silvanos were working through the wizards with ties to the Council, looking for the hidden elemental fragments.

It was no coincidence that I was standing in the Belore house. It was a piece of the puzzle.

I TRIED AGAIN to lift the mirror off the wall, but it wouldn't budge. It was an excellent place to hide something, because when you looked at it you saw yourself and your brain automatically went: *that's not what we're searching for. Good hair, though.*

The amulet urged me to move closer to the glass, and I did as prompted. I moved closer and closer, till my breath misted up the mirror and the Dragon's Eye was once again burning my palm. Closer, till my body was pressed up against it. And then when I put my forehead to the cool glass, and my nose, and my lips, as if I meant to kiss my mirror-twin, it started to soften. Slowly at first, it melted around me, becoming a mercury membrane that I was being allowed to pass through. I held my breath and stepped through the mirror.

IF I HAD BEEN EXPECTING Wonderland on the other side, I would have been sorely disappointed. Instead of a vaping caterpillar and an insane hat-maker, there was just a very small, dark, room. It was, however, far superior to Wonderland in one way: it was lit by incredibly beautiful blue lightning, which was pulsing inside a large jar that stood on a pedestal in the center. I tried to take a step and almost fell over. The floor was like black Jell-O. It was a safety measure, I guessed, in case the Jar fell off its platform. With the dark jelly there it wouldn't break if it fell to the ground, it wouldn't even bounce. The slurping gelatin would embrace it like a big wobbly Jell-O mama monster. With substantial effort, I made my way towards the Jar, and when it was within reach, I took it from its platform.

That's when the alarm sounded. Of course it did; what was I expecting? That I could just smash and grab one of the most potent and dangerous magical items in the Realm?

So, maybe I hadn't thought the whole thing through, but you could hardly blame me. I was running on fear and adrenaline. I had nothing else in my tank. I felt like lying down in that strange black Jell-O and giving up. But as the alarm screeched in my ears I thought of Musubarin, and the Ember Isles. Boulderkeep labor colony, and the Black Tower, and that gave me the energy to move. I slipped the Chaos Jar into my infinity pocket and pushed my way back through the quicksilver film.

When I stepped back into the Belore bedroom I heard tires squeal on the road outside, and saw the blue flashing lights: an impromptu disco party. Even if Tilexon wasn't in one of those cars down there, I thought, peeking through the blinds, he'd be minutes away. I wasn't about to repeat the trauma of my first arrest. I needed to get out of there. I watched as two of the officers started banging down the pedestrian gate. I wished I could use my portal key. I wished I could summon my bike. I wished I could turn myself invisible, but I could no longer do any of those things. I squeezed my eyes shut for a moment, cursing the volt cuff and forcing myself to think. There was another bang and my eyes clicked open again. They had broken down the gate and were inside the property. They had left all three cars on the road, doors open, lights flashing.

And I would have bet my pet ferret that at least one of those SUVs still had the key in the ignition.

CHAPTER 16
HASTA LA VISTA

I heard the officers' boots thudding on the timber floors below. I looked up at the ceiling, looking for an entrance to the roof cavity. The ceiling was smooth, so I ran into the bathroom, and then to the office, where I found a barely-there square of ceiling board that looked like it could be my ticket out. I heard a pair of feet running up the stairs, so I quickly closed and locked the office door, and shoved Ametrix's heavy desk against it. As I scraped it across the floor, a framed picture of the Belore family fell off the edge. I scooped it up and put it in my pocket. A gift for the twins.

The officer pounded on the door.

"She's here!" he yelled down to the others. "Upstairs!"

I stood on the arm of the couch and reached up, using my wand to dislodge the small square board in the ceiling.

Once I had managed to move it out of the way, I climbed down again and moved to the farthest corner of the office. I took a breath, readied my muscles, then sprinted back to the couch, jumping and using the arm as a springboard to leap up and grab onto the edges of the door.

I hung there for a moment, catching my breath. My fingers were hurting from the strain of carrying the weight of my whole body. There was another bang, this time right in my ears, as the uniforms outside the office started to bash down the door. With gargantuan effort, and a groan to go with it, I pulled myself up. It was too difficult. I tried twice and failed twice, and then my arm muscles decided they didn't want to try anymore.

Deodamnatus.

On an ordinary day I would have been able to do this, but I had missed a few training sessions recently. I wasn't too hard on myself. It wasn't due to lack of willpower. It was due to trying to stay alive, and keeping other people alive, dodging evil orcs and goblin gangsters. Not to mention the vampires who kept me on my toes. Still, none of this helped my situation, I thought, as I hung from the tips of my fingers, and my hands began to cramp.

I let go, and fell onto the couch. There was an almighty bash against the door and the wood splintered. They were seconds away from snapping on those handcuffs again, which I wouldn't be able to bear. I'd rather die, I thought. I'd rather die fighting here than be hauled off to SubT again. That gave me an idea. I ran to the window and wrenched open the curtains. Turns out it wasn't a window at all, but a glass door that led out onto a little balcony. I smashed open the bolt and dashed outside into the cool night air. I jumped up onto the guard rail, then dropped, swinging from it to land on the ground below, which was cushioned with plants.

I landed with an "*Oof!*" and an apology to the hydrangeas, which I'm sure were wondering what they had done to deserve such treatment. I pulled a stray stick out of my hair as I snuck around the building, back to the wall. The fortunate thing about the cops all being upstairs, bashing down a door, is that I could run undetected through the yard, back through the house, and out the front gate.

As it happened, all three of the SUVs had keys in their ignitions, so I could take my pick. I chose the one on the end that looked ready and waiting for a quick getaway. But before I climbed in, I reached into cars one and two, swiped the keys, and threw them over the neighbor's wall.

Hasta la vista, escorpiones.

If you're wondering how a Jo'burg girl learned how to speak such good Spanish, I'll tell you. I grew up watching reruns of *The Terminator* and *Dora the Explorer*.

I jumped into the third car, slammed the door, and twisted the key. The engine came to life, and as I tried to remember how to drive, I smashed the accelerator down and jumped forward. I was making it up as I was going along, and as the car took off under my inexpert control, quite possibly leaving a skid mark on the road, I heard shouting from the house. I flattened the pedal to the floor and we flew forward. As I glimpsed in the rearview mirror the uniforms running out onto the road, I felt like I could breathe again. I turned the corner and accelerated. Cars always felt a bit claustrophobic to me, but without a bike or a portal key, I had the feeling that having that SUV was going to come in very handy.

I CONSIDERED STOPPING somewhere to remove the plates, but then realized it would be a waste of time. The car would have anti-theft tech anyway, plus there was the tracking chip in my cuff. Musubarin could find me (or electrocute me) at any time, but for some reason he was letting me run. I wasn't going to ask why. The radio crackled and fizzed, then a voice came over the sound system. There was a security breach at the Carlton Centre, the woman said. A raging fire at the Ponte Tower, and an armed robbery at Goblin City. All available officers were required.

The world was going mad, I thought. I had a sudden jab of empathy for the police force, and for the Scorpions. Hearing this kind of news day in and day out must take its toll. The woman's voice made me think of Morgan, and how Musubarin's heavies had dragged her out of the Scorpion HQ as if she was a crazy woman instead of the best detective that unit had ever seen. Because of me, she had first been demoted, and then fired. I felt terrible about it. I wanted to see her, speak to her, tell her everything, but first, I had something important to do.

ONCE I WAS BACK in the city, I pulled over and jumped out of the car.

I had the Chaos Jar.

I had the Chaos Jar, and everything was going to be fine. Relatively speaking. Because not only did I have the Jar, but I also had a plan. If the fulfillment of the New Dawn prophecy depended on bringing together the three elemental fragments, then I had to do everything in my power to stop that from happening. You might think that I should have left the Jar where it was, because it was safer there, behind the magic mirror, than it was in my pocket. And *I* was certainly safer without it, because I knew from my experience with the HighFire Crown that keeping a magical item in your infinity pocket was a sure way to attract all kinds of dangerous creatures. But I also knew that as long as the Jar was hidden in the Belore house, the Silvanos would keep kidnapping and torturing wizards with any kind of ties to the Council until one spilled the magic beans, and I wasn't going to let that happen. Besides, knowing the Jar was out there, out of my control, made me feel intensely uncomfortable. It was a vulnerability the Realm could ill afford.

I took the Chaos Jar out of my pocket and looked at it. White lightning struck the bottom and sides over and over again, sending out flashes of incredible blue light. Watching it bolt and flicker, I thought that if magic ever had a symbol, a picture, to epitomize it, it would be this blue lightning. Even though I was cut off from the Void, I could feel the magic in the Jar; I could sense its potential power.

It was one of the most beautiful things I had ever seen, I thought, as I turned it in my hands. A part of me wanted to keep it forever, but my survival instinct reared up and told me to get back to work. Do what I was supposed to do. I took one last longing look at the Jar, and smashed it down onto the hard black tarmac below.

CHAPTER 17

BLACK HONEY

The glass didn't shatter, as I had expected it to. I thought it would be fragile, taking into account the way it had been so carefully protected in its little safe room. I bent down and picked it up, ready to try again, but this time I'd really put some muscle behind it.

If I destroyed the Chaos Jar it would be impossible to unite the three elemental fragments, and the prophecy would die a small, sad, silent death. Maybe it would whimper a little, but only if you kicked it.

I held the Jar in both hands now, ready to hurl it as hard as I could onto the ground below, when something strange happened. Some of the blue light from inside the Jar started to leak out, like blue mist. When I looked closer, I saw that I had in fact cracked the glass on the first attempt, but it was just a tiny hairline fracture. It would be barely noticeable if not for the wisp of cerulean smoke.

That wasn't the strange part. The strange part was that when I looked at the sky and expected to see the usual black of night speckled with stars, there was something else up there, too. At first it looked like the trail of a shooting star—if shooting stars were able to travel across more than half the visible sky—and then I realized the shape of the shimmering gash was exactly the same as the hairline crack in the Jar.

What. The. Faex.

Was there a crack in the sky? I wondered. A *crack* in the *sky*?

I knew it wasn't possible, but there was no denying that the line was identical to the one in the Jar I held in my hands. It was as if we were in a giant snow globe, and the glass bubble had been fissured. Not enough for all the water and glitter to escape—or not yet anyway—but enough to show us that we were in trouble. So much trouble.

Oh my faex, I thought, my nerves spiking my brain.

Had I just broken the Realm?

IT MADE me remember the time my orc security guard, Gnor, had accidentally dislocated my shoulder (don't ask). The way he had looked at me then, like a child who had accidentally broken his toy.

Did I break the wizard? I could practically hear him thinking. *Uh oh.*

I was sure my face, right then, mirrored his horrified expression. Except that I hadn't broken a toy or a wizard. I seem to have broken the entire *faexing* Realm.

Holy, holy hex.

It's okay, I tried to tell myself. *Don't panic. It's just a giant slash of silver in space. It's quite pretty, really, the way it shimmers like that. Nice to look at.*

But I wasn't fooling anyone. I knew it was bad. I knew it was Very, Very Bad.

I looked down at the Jar again, wishing it would just heal itself. The Void knows that even if I hadn't lost my magic I wouldn't have tried to heal the Jar. Too risky. Once I had tried to fix my magical crossbow with a healing spell and it did not turn out well.

I looked at the Jar, then back up at the sky, then back at the Jar. I was using all the power I had to A) Not Panic; and B) Think of a Plan. Neither was going very well.

MAYBE DARICK COULD FIX the Jar, I thought, desperately. He was the best healer I knew. I wasn't sure if his talent applied to inanimate objects, but it would be worth a try, right? He had done good job of fixing Slyden Abarim's voodoo doll.

But I didn't know where Darick was, and I couldn't phone him, because he had given me his mobile, which was sitting on my rickety kitchen table at home.

I thought of taking the Jar to Ferra. She would know what to do. But the painful truth was that I didn't even know if Ferra was alive. I don't know how much damage the gas explosion at *The Copper Cog* had done. I had to haul my thoughts away from my favorite dwarf and focus on my predicament.

It was difficult to think, because I had a strange buzzing in my ears, as if a swarm of insects were passing over me. When I glanced in the direction of the sound, I saw that there were actually bees in the air. They looked black in the dark of the night, but they were definitely bees. Black bees made me think of black honey, and the air like molasses at EverShade, and my heart started climbing up my throat.

I was no apiologist, but I knew that bees didn't swarm about randomly at night time. One of the animals landed on the back of my hand. I lifted it up, slowly, so that I could get a proper look at it, and as I watched, it lowered its thorax to my skin and injected me with its poison.

"Ah!" I exclaimed, more in surprise than pain, although it did sting like a *filius canis*. I shook my hand and the little apian bastard flew away to join his friends, as if nothing had happened. As if we lived in a world where bees could sting out of spite and not receive the death penalty for doing so. I narrowed my eyes at the shadow swarm as it moved away, then walked slowly to the squad car, wondering if the insects were a bad omen, or worse. I climbed into the vehicle and shut the door, feeling immediately safer. The bulletproof exterior of the car could protect me from some things, at least. I put my hands on the wheel and watched as the skin on my hand swelled.

CHAPTER 18
PLANES DON'T JUST DROP OUT OF THE SKY

The drive towards Morgan's house was interesting. Black bees had nothing on the kinds of things I saw on that trip. First of all, the untouched people were still acting like zombies, except now they seemed more dangerous than before. They were certainly more terrifying to look at. They all had those silver irises and deeply bloodshot eyes. Their masks of indifference leaned more towards aggression than before: clenched jaws, furrowed brows, faces set in vicious snarls. I didn't see any of them act violently, but having observed their transformation I knew that it was just a matter of time. And they still seemed to be severely visually and mentally impaired, walking into things like blind zombies.

It was horrifying to see people like that, and the woman on the police car radio felt the same way. She remained professional but I could hear the strain in her voice, the tremor. She felt like the Realm was collapsing around her, and she wasn't wrong. I imagined her having a young family at home, and feeling desperate to get to them and protect them, but her duty as a dispatcher was just as important. *That's the problem with having children*, I thought. It's like you had to divide your heart into pieces and then let those pieces go out into the world, which was a perilous place. Had to watch those hearts beat without you, and pray that they kept on beating, because if they died, a piece of you would die, too.

I knew I'd never have children. Firstly, I found it difficult enough to feed and clothe myself. As I've mentioned before, I can't even keep the cockroaches in my kitchen alive. But that aside, I knew I wouldn't be able to deal with that kind of vulnerability. When my parents died, I wanted to die, too. It was like I had bled out along with them, bled till I was empty and cold, and I'd never been able to get warm again. I couldn't go through that again, and I certainly didn't want my imaginary children to have to. Not that I'd ever have the chance to procreate, anyway, I thought, as I looked out of the smoked glass window of the SUV, because outside looked like apocalypse city on acid.

I stopped at a flashing traffic light, although I needn't have bothered. I was driving the only car on the road. The robot wasn't just flashing red, though. It was alternating colors as if it were sending a Morse code, a rainbow SOS. A man walked straight into my fender, fell down, then got back up and walked in a different direction. Music started to blare from the SUV's speakers. It was that goblin punk rock band, The Klash, and their screeches clawed at my ears. I tried to turn the noise off, but the radio had other ideas. I opened my window, hoping to mitigate the racket, and the bitter, bright, acrid stink of the city streamed into the car. I saw a tree grow extra roots, smashing through the concrete pavers below and upending a bench. Lights on billboards and inside skyscrapers flickered, and if the current feeding them was unstable.

I put my foot down. I had to get to Morgan. Morgan was a muggle—as she affectionately referred to untouched people like herself after a few pints—and as far as I could see, this silver-eye disease, this brain-deleting zombification was contagious. A Possession Plague. I needed to get to my best friend before she caught it, too.

I had seen the looted shops before, and the burning wreckage. And the zombies. But, now, with that fracture in the sky, things took on a slightly different tint. Something was spilling out of that crack and causing havoc within the city. In the distance, I watched as a plane swooped down and crashed to the ground below, sending up an explosion of smoke and flames. It was so surreal I thought I must be dreaming, but as I watched the fire burn, I felt like I couldn't breathe, felt like I couldn't drag any air into my lungs. Planes don't just drop out of the sky. Then I understood what that gash in the night sky was. It was a Void fracture, and all the wild magic of the Void was leaking into the Realm.

CHAPTER 19
JUST WATCHING THE STARS

On the way over to Morgan's house I felt like the world was crashing down around me. Plants snaked across the road, fires burned with purple flames, and the moon looked tinged with red.

Holy faex, holy faex, holy faex, I kept thinking. *What have I done?*

I couldn't see how life could get any worse. My magic was gone, the Realm was crumbling, and it was all my fault.

I sped across the city to where Morgan lived in a high security complex. The roads were eerily quiet, and every time I leaned forward in my stolen vehicle to glance at the sky, I saw that terrible fracture in the night. When I arrived at the complex, I assumed the guards would stop me and ask me for the usual: my weapons, driver's license, digital fingerprint, retina scan, DNA sample, and a virgin goat sacrifice. But it was worse than that, and my stomach plummeted. There were no guards on duty, and the gate had been forced open. I didn't stop to look for their bodies. I didn't need another reminder that we were all waiting in a rather fast-moving queue to meet Mr. Reaper.

I put my foot down again, and was grateful for the SUV: its eager acceleration, armored exterior, and run-flat tires. But any feeling of fortune quickly evaporated when I screeched into Morgan's driveway. The security complex was usually a pretty cheerful place, with its smooth wide roads and landscaped gardens. Even at night there were usually signs of life: lights twinkling, teenagers' televisions blaring, the sounds of cooking and dinner conversations. But that night, there was nothing. It was a ghost town.

I walked up the paved pathway toward Morgan's door. I saw that it was slightly ajar, and the hairs on the back of my neck stood up.

"Morgan?" I called.

I pushed open the door and called again, but no one was home. It felt at that moment as if there was not one other living human being on the entire estate. I walked through to her kitchen, flicking the light switches, but there was no power. Had the Hammerskins blown up the substation here, like they had done in Samantha Farzad's suburb, or had the Void fracture blown the lightbulbs? Not that it mattered. Morgan was missing, her kids were missing, and I feared the worst.

I turned to leave, and as I did so I caught a glimpse of color in my peripheral vision. I stopped. Slowly, quietly, I took a couple of tentative steps in the direction of the movement I thought I had seen, my lungs ballooning. I crept along, looking for whatever it was. The house was dark, and I missed my *illuminos* spell. I also missed my utility belt, which had my penlight in it. Although, to be fair, I never replaced the batteries in the thing so it probably would have died in my hands anyway.

I searched for a while longer, but I didn't find anything. I moved to the kitchen and searched Morgan's cupboards and drawers for one of her flashlights. Morgan was the kind of person who always made sure her kitchen was stocked, her fuel tank full, and that her flashlights had charged batteries. She was born with the *Successful Adulting* gene, the one I never got. To underscore my belief, the next drawer I pulled out had a great big flashlight. It was the heavy duty kind, and when I clicked the glow-in-the-dark button to switch it on, the beam of light appeared, strong and steady.

Not one to miss out on an opportunity, I raided her snack cupboard, too. I grabbed a box of protein bars for myself, and bag of biltong for Gizmo. My anxiety for my missing friend had crushed my appetite, but I figured they may come in handy during the apocalypse.

On my second attempt to leave the house, I walked out of the front door and down the path, but again something stopped me. There was the sound of running water behind the hedge. It was coming from Liz Durison's house. I peered over the plants, sweeping the flashlight over the front of her house. When I shone the light on the lawn, I jumped. My heart sprinted at what I saw.

Liz Durison was lying there, naked, her face pointed to the sky. I felt the black mist then, exactly as Morgan had felt it the night she had discovered her neighbor's body. There was evil in the air. Everything I looked at seemed tainted with malice. I scrambled around the hedge and onto Durison's property. When I reached her body she sat up and smiled, making me jump again.

"Filius canis, Durison," I said, grabbing at my chest, sure I was about to have a heart attack. "What are you doing out here?"

She looked into my eyes. Her irises had decayed; her skin was slack. "Just watching the stars," she said.

I looked at the "V" symbol branded on her chest. I expected her to nag me again about finding her killer, but she didn't. She seemed to be in some kind of trance. Perhaps she had given up on me. She lay back down on the black grass and stared at the sky.

I wanted to apologize, but how do you say sorry for something like that?

I'm sorry I never found your killer.

I'm sorry your kids lost their mother.

I'm sorry you're stuck in some kind of weird limbo where you never get any peace.

Then she turned her head slightly to look at me again. Her neck made a crunching sound.

"It's all a bit backwards," she said. "Isn't it?"

If she meant the Void Fracture, then, yes, I suppose she was right. Everything was out of balance. And the more the wild magic leaked into the Realm, the more havoc it would cause.

I LEFT Liz Durison's ghost there, naked, on the cold lawn. Guilt turned my stomach to stone, and the anxiety I felt for Morgan frayed my thoughts, making it difficult to think of a plan of action. I jumped back into the car and slammed the door. That's when I saw a missed call on my phone.

Morgan.

Relief gushed through me. Morgan had not caught the Possession Plague. Yet.

I tried to call her back, but it just went to voicemail. After trying twice more with no luck, I clicked on the message she sent me. Her voice was strained, and I battled to hear what she was saying over the static on the line, which kept breaking up.

"Jax ... Jax," she said. "Do not see ... again. Do not trust ... not safe. I think ... I know ... who killed Liz Durison."

CHAPTER 20
THE GREEDY TENDRIL

I hightailed it back to my apartment. I had nowhere else to go, and I thought if Morgan would meet me anywhere, it would be there. I needed an hour in a safe place to calm my nerves and to think. I needed to figure out how I was going to fix the colossal mess I had made. With all the traffic lights on the blink and the streets empty it was easy to speed home. I knocked a couple of trashcans over and flattened a few cardboard boxes on my way. The cabin of the SUV seemed to lose its claustrophobic quality once I reached a certain speed.

I parked in the basement and raced up the stairs. It wouldn't have been my first choice, but the Swift was out of order. I arrived at my front door gasping and sweating and congratulating myself for not keeling over.

I gave Gizmo some biltong to eat, offloading a good portion of it into his snack bowl in his Ferret Dreamhouse, then sat down at my toothpick-legged table and picked up a banana from the fruit basket. It was the only thing I thought I could stomach. I peeled it and started to eat, but the bites were difficult to swallow, and I gave up halfway. A cold breeze moved past me, and I shivered.

"Hello, Ghost," I said. I was in a world of pain, but at least I had Ghost. The idea of the comfort I would feel in freshly laundered clothes appealed to me, so I left the table and walked to my bedroom, where my bed was clean and perfectly made up. Pity I didn't have time to rest.

I pulled off my stinky pajamas and turned on the shower. The pipes in the wall groaned and hissed, and banged around.

That doesn't sound good, I thought, but I didn't turn it off. When the water finally came through it was brown and had flecks of black in it that looked like dead ants. I ran it for a little longer, hoping it would run clear, but the color just got darker. I turned it off and opted for deodorant, instead. The idea of those black flecks in my hair and on my scalp made my skin crawl.

BACK AT THE kitchen table I sorted through the mess that had accumulated there. I put Darick's phone and gun to one side, then, on second thoughts, I pocketed the gun. I wasn't usually a fan of firearms but the loss of my magic had changed the game. Behind Darick's bag of personal belongings was Kruq's, the gray-skinned goblin. I zipped open the plastic bag and immediately regretted it. The stench of his clothes was on par with really ripe, veiny orc cheese. I had to lean over, away from the bag, and stop myself from retching. When the urge to vomit passed, I pulled out the garment that was so smelly and threw it out the window.

Usually, littering really bothers me. I've been known to stop people on the street and tell them to pick up their trash. But there was no way I could have that thing in my home, not even in the garbage Who knows which kind of invisible insects were teeming in that rough hessian cloth, or what kind of germs? Nope. Now it could join the dumpster fire outside where it belonged.

There were two other items in the goblin's bag. A tarnished silver coin with a fancy emblem on it, and a small bottle of sleeping draught. I pocketed them both. You never know when these things could come in handy.

ONCE I'D CLEARED the table, I stood there and stared at the jungle that was slowly eating my home. I wondered when the forest animals would start moving in: tarantulas, anacondas, golden gibbons. Wondered how long it would take for them to colonize the whole apartment, the whole building, the whole city. It would be an improvement. Like those pictures of wrecked, war-torn places where the wildlife has covered the burnt carcasses of cars and abandoned homes.

I found the kitchen counter—a small part that wasn't covered in leaves—and leaned on it, thinking about what to do next. I felt something tickle my fingers and I jumped and moved away, the idea of tarantulas still looming in my imagination. But it wasn't a spider, it was a greedy tendril of the plant. It was snaking over the small area as if sniffing for food. My nerves prickled against my skin, as if the plant had bitten me, and I hugged my hand to my chest, feeling repulsed. I thought of the black flecks in the dirty water and the ravenous plant and I had the strong urge to get out of there. I pulled on my trench coat, grabbed my things—including an extra muffin—and fled down the stairs.

CHAPTER 21
RUM & MAPLE

The problem with using a summoning spell to call your motorbike is that you don't always pay attention to where you park it. I never even thought about where I parked my bike because I knew I couldn't lose it. When I got down to the parking basement of my building, it wasn't there. I automatically reached for my summoning ring from Ferra, and then swore at myself. So much of my life was automatic magic, I didn't even realize how much I depended on it for everyday living. Luckily, I still had the stolen Scorpion SUV.

I jumped into the car and clipped in my seat belt, checking my mirrors as I did so.

"Hello, Ms. Knight," said the man in the back seat, and I almost catapulted out of the roof.

"Filius canis," I gasped, clutching my chest. "You gave me such a fright."

"Sincerest apologies," he said. The white smoke he wore drifted around him like a nest of slow-moving snakes. I gulped down my anxiety, unclipped my belt, and turned around to look at the deadling djinn in the eyes.

"What the *faex* are you doing here? Shouldn't you be playing happy half-dead family in limbo land?"

Alif steepled his hands. "I came here to make good on my promise to you."

That made me sit up straight. Was Alif going to tell me about my parents? I started breathing harder.

Alif saw the hope on my face and patted down his smoke with his palms, as if trying to lower my expectations. "Or, half-good, anyway."

I scratched my temple. "Half-good?"

"I have information for you, but it's not the information you crave."

"You djinni," I said, irritated. "So damn slippery." I knew the smoke was an illusion, but it made me cough, anyway.

Alif waited for me to stop, then he continued. "I know you want to know about yourself. Your real name. Your parents."

"Yes."

"But I have something else for you. Something more ... pressing."

I was impatient, drumming my hands on my lap. What was he waiting for?

"Land the plane, djinni. I've got things to do."

The djinn clicked his fingers, and a cigarette appeared. He blew gently on the tip to light it, and the tobacco glowed a golden orange and scented the cabin with rum and maple.

"Samantha told you how I died."

"Not really. She didn't know the details. Said it was covered up."

I rolled down the windows to allow the imaginary smoke to escape.

"But she told you that I was a spy. For the Council."

"Yes," I said, and I stopped fidgeting. I wanted to hear this. I'd never met a spy before.

"It was covered up because I was working on a sensitive case when it happened."

"All Council cases are sensitive," I said. "What made this one special?"

When he didn't answer me, I glared at him.

"You," he said.

I felt as if I had the wind knocked out of me. Struck airless and speechless, I just blinked at him.

"What?" I finally said.

"You were the reason the case was sensitive."

Eloquence flew out the car window along with the imaginary cigarette smoke. "What?" I said again. "I don't understand. The Council doesn't even know I exist."

Alif looked surprised at that. "Oh, yes, they do."

I felt like I'd been hit by a truck and all my body parts had been rearranged. My brain was lying on the ground, my heart stopped beating. Nothing was making sense and everything hurt.

"I don't understand," I said again. "What part did I play in the case you were investigating?"

Alif laughed, the cigarette smoke cascading out of his mouth and rushing to join the sparking clouds that swirled around him.

"What part did you play in the case?" he said. "Ms. Knight. You *were* the case."

My brain still lay on the ground, useless.

"Why?" I asked.

"Look," he said. "I can't tell you as much as I'd like to. I'm sworn to secrecy. You'd think I'd be out of the Council's reach, being half-specter. But I know from personal experience that they can reach you anywhere. And I have a family to look after."

I felt angry then.

"So you thought you'd just come and drop this on my lap with no explanation and then disappear again."

"I thought you'd rather know," he said.

He was right, and that made me angrier. Angry and totally useless. It occurred to me how pointless an emotion anger is when you can't channel it to create magic. Like pain, and guilt. I saw no use in emotions if you couldn't transform them into light.

"How did you die?" I asked.

"I'll spare you the bloody details," he said. "But it had a happy ending. My love for Samantha kept me alive enough to latch on to the magic that was swirling around me when it happened."

"But who killed you? And how is it related to me?"

"You'll find out," he said. "They don't call you the best wizard detective in the city for nothing."

"There must be something else you can tell me," I said. "Please."

Then it was his turn to stare at me. He didn't blink, which reminded me of Morgan, who was still missing. I thought of Ferra, too. It turned a screw in my heart.

"The reason I came to tell you this was not for the sake of information itself, but to warn you," he said.

"I appreciate that," I said through a clenched jaw. "But what exactly are you warning me about? The person who killed you? Does the Council know who it was?"

"You won't want to hear it from me," he said. "You'll have to discover it for yourself. But I had to warn you ... it's someone close to you."

The deadling djinn started to fade away.

"So take extra care, wizard. Nothing is as it seems."

"Damn it, Alif," I said. "Just tell me! Tell me who killed you!"

But he was already gone, and only the faintest wisp of rum and maple smoke remained.

CHAPTER 22
JUST GRIN AND BE VULNERABLE

Cursing in every ancient language I could think of, I shoved the key into its slot and turned it. The SUV's engine roared as I fed it fuel, and it felt good. Alif's visit had infuriated me, but at least it had given me an idea of where to go. The cracked Chaos Jar pulsated in my pocket as if it were a living thing. It was too dangerous for me to hang on to the thing, and I couldn't destroy it. There was only one thing left to do.

I put my foot down and raced through the city, which was behaving just as strangely as before, with its zombie pedestrians and dead streetlights. Buildings flickered on and off, and the fracture in the sky glimmered silver and white. I had to slow down because there were dogs on the road. One or two wouldn't have raised an eyebrow, but there were dozens, and they didn't look like strays. There were cats, too. All different colors and breeds. I assumed the pets had escaped from their homes when their owners turned into walking corpses. But they weren't acting like dogs. They weren't fighting or cowering in their unfamiliar environment. The all looked totally at ease, as if they owned the streets; I couldn't help thinking that it was a vast improvement. My imagination leapt to ideas of canines and felines reigning over the city and making all the rules. First on the list for cats would be to build in more free time to lie around in the sun, which I approved of. Dogs would push for more time to play, and more treats. Again, it was a party I would vote for.

I didn't see any Hammerskins on the drive. At first I was relieved, but it also made me wonder where they were and what they were up to. A stark absence of Neo-Nazi orcs and their bloodthirsty bosses, the Silvanos, gave me a sensation of dread so deep it froze my spine. I knew I needed to find them, find out what they were doing and put a stop to it, but as I felt the pressure of the volt cuff on my ankle I wondered how I would do it. One thing was for sure: without access to the Void, the odds were not stacked in my favor.

The Jar continued to glow in my pocket as I pulled into the parking lot of the The Winged Spire, the parliament tower that housed the Council and all the administrative teams that made it work. It was late at night, and the parking lot was deserted, but there were some lights on in the top floor, where the Council pillars had their seats. There was a saying in the Realm: *The Council Never Sleeps*. It was true, practically and metaphorically. It meant that no matter what, the Council was there, all-seeing, all-knowing, like a living thing that surrounds its people, keeping them safe and making sure that everyone behaves in the correct way. But the literal meaning was true, too, because the Council Wizards worked in shifts that overlapped one after the other, so that there were, at all times, wakeful wizards to deal with whatever challenges the Realm threw at them. Every few hours, one of the wizards would come to relieve the wizard who had started their duty twelve hours before. Then the next wizard would arrive, and so on. I closed the car door and looked up at the skyscraper offices lit by incandescent bulbs. There was, at any time, at least four wizards on duty. And not just any wizards. The Council pillars were the most respected in the country. Honest, ethical, fair, and generally just beyond reproach. The Council would know what to do with the Chaos Jar.

I WALKED UP to the entrance, which was guarded by Khargol orcs. They looked on edge. No doubt they had seen the effects of the wild magic that was leaking out of the Void. I felt sorry for them. Ousted by blunt-brained skinheads—which can't be good for anyone's ego—and forced to submit to their cold-blooded leader, Raguk Magra, who was known for killing entire families of dissidents and displaying their decapitated heads on spikes outside their houses as a warning to bend the knee or die. Their bodies were dumped in mass graves in the further parts of the SubRealm and covered with fine mining dust there. No mercy was granted to frail or vulnerable orcs: senior citizens; children; sick or disabled people. If they had a heartbeat, it could be stopped. I had seen the gut-wrenching pictures on Forage news, pictures so brutal they'd be burnt into your brain for years. The ruthlessness of the campaign had ensured Magra had no rebel forces take up arms against him. Orcs were generally pretty vile creatures, but they did put family first, and most of them wouldn't jeopardize their babies' lives by resisting the orc version of Idi Amin.

I nodded to the guards as they frisked me and found nothing. I had left Darick's gun in the glove compartment of the car, as well as my crossbow. Gizmo was at home. I didn't like walking around unarmed, with no way to sling spells, but it was the only way to get into the Spire.

I would have to just grin and be vulnerable. At least I was on home ground.

CHAPTER 23
A RED DWARF DUMPLING

"I.D.," said the grumpy looking goblin at the desk. She ignored the three phones at her elbow that were ringing off the hook. I was surprised; I thought the phone lines were down. Behind me, the reception area was lined with worried looking creatures, as if this was a hospital waiting room instead of the seat of parliament. Her rubbery lips were crimped together over her toothpick teeth and I couldn't help thinking it must hurt. Her mouth was painted a deep, glossy shade of bacon that made her lips look like raw meat, as if the skin had been stripped off them. I looked away, but then forced myself to look at her again. I focused on her bulging eyes, instead.

"My wallet was stolen," I said. "I don't have an I.D. I haven't had time to go to Realm Affairs yet."

She pursed her pork strips. She was not impressed and wanted me to know all about it.

"You can't come in here without an I.D.," she said.

I didn't have time for red tape. The universe was folding down around us and I had the cause in my pocket.

"And even if you had an I.D., you'd be—" she squinted at the small ticket machine in front of her. "Number three hundred and sixty-two in the queue."

"If you give me a number I'll wait," I said.

The goblin sighed. "There's something else," she said. "The queue isn't moving."

"At all?"

"At all. Have you been outside?" she asked. "The wizards don't have time to deal with this—" she gestured at the muttering people. She leaned in and whispered. "They're trying to stop the end of the world."

The goblin slid her pencil behind her ear, into the greasy tundra that passed for hair on goblins' heads. "Besides, you'll never get in. Have you seen how many people are here?"

I looked back again, then nodded. "They're keeping you busy." I said. "Coming here with their problems. Blocking up the system."

She had a funny expression, as if she wanted to say "*Preach!*" and high-five the heavens.

"What if I told you that I have something that will help the Council solve all of this," I pointed at the crowd behind me.

"I'd say you're not very good at lying," she said, bearing her dirty toothpicks. "But I do appreciate your creative thinking."

"Seriously," I said. "I know why this is all happening, and I really need to see the Council about it."

"I told you, honey," she said. "They're not seeing anyone right now. They're trying to stop the universe from imploding. They haven't even eaten their dinners tonight. I ordered their favorite. Sashimi salad and dumplings from Red Dwarf. They didn't even touch it. I had to order a fresh round."

"If you could just tell them who I am," I said. "I think they'd be willing to see me."

The goblin laughed. "No offense, sweetheart, you're something to look at. Might even have some brain cells. But you're no match for a Red Dwarf dumpling."

Frustration began to gnaw at me. I wasn't going to get past this pork-lipped Grinch.

Then I remembered something Pepin Belore said to me when we were trying to hack into Musubarin's computer.

"You're trying to get in the front door," she had said. She had, of course, found her way through the back door.

I left the entrance of the building. Before going past the guards again, I took advantage of their turned backs and wended my way along the exterior of the building, around two corners, and to the back of the tower. It was huge and it took me a while to get to where I wanted to be.

It was late, and the usually bustling service entrance was dark and quiet, apart from a Red Dwarf delivery van parked in one of the solar carports, just out of view of the guards. I could imagine during the day that area would be buzzing with cars and delivery bikes. Laundry; sanitary; waste; water. Sashimi and dumplings.

I cursed the volt cuff again. Without it, I could have turned my coat invisible and snuck past the guards on duty. Instead, under the cover of dark, I crept up to the food van —still warm—and checked that there was no one in the front. Then I took a clip out of my hair, straightened it, and inserted it into the lock of the passenger door. After a few attempts—my fingers were trembling, and slippery with sweat—the silver mechanism clicked and the door unlocked. I squeezed my eyes shut as I levered open the door, expecting a shrill siren from the car alarm, but there was just a happy silence. I thanked the Void and slid into the car, climbing over the chair to access the restaurant goods at the back. Using Morgan's flashlight, I found the things I needed, and when I climbed out of the delivery van again I was all set to break into the most hallowed building in the Realm.

CHAPTER 24

SEARED FLESH SCENTED FLASHBACKS

Instead of sneaking past the guards at the back of the building, I decided to walk up to them and introduce myself instead. They were bristling with automatic weapons so I decided it was best to meet them face-to-face instead of risking being caught breaking in. What I really wished for was a glamour potion, so that I could pass for a Red Dwarf, but my luck was only stretching so far.

"Aben, aben," I said, in my best Dwarven. *Good evening.*

The orcs looked at my get-up: a Japanese gown that came to my shins and a red sash over my shoulder with golden tassels. The apron was emblazoned with the Red Dwarf logo: a dumpling with a Viking hat wielding red chopsticks.

The guards blinked their weary eyes.

"What doing?" asked the first orc, letting go of his gun to scratch his chin.

"Fresh dumplings," I said. "And sashimi."

"Already delivered," said the other orc.

"Oh," I said, frowning.

"Someone else already delivered," he said again. "Take them aw—"

"I'm going to get into so much trouble," I said. "Messing up like this on my first day. I can't take these back. They'll fire me."

I forced myself to cry; it was easier than I expected. All I had to do was remember *The Copper Cog* and tears sprang to my eyes.

They both stared at me, hands on their guns that shone silver under the security lights.

"You can leave them with us," said the second orc, the one with a potbelly that would have made a laughing Buddha proud. "We'll take them up."

"Thank you!" I said. "Thank you very much."

The second orc did a bad job of hiding his smile. "Yes, we'll take it up."

I left the platter with them and walked back to the van.

· · ·

FIVE MINUTES later I returned to find the pair of orcs passed out on the tarmac, and the half-eaten dumplings scattered on the ground beside them. I stole their access cards, dragged their bodies out of sight—which was no mean feat as they were the weight of baby elephants—and then raced into the building.

A fortnight before I had visited the orc SubRealm. I'd gotten my glamour on as a pickle-face and visited the beer hall looking for clues on a case I had been working on. I knew someone wanted the Orc Godfather—Don Vito—dead, but I'd needed to find out who, and why. On edge, and distracted by the cage fighting in the corner, I had accepted a beer from a skinhead. Next thing I knew, I was dragged, unconscious, to a dark corner of the hall, where Zargulg, the Hammerskin, tried to assault me. Long story short, I used my fury to barbecue his nipple. That turned out to be the least of his problems when I bumped into him again a few days later. I still get seared flesh scented flashbacks, which I try to forget, but I did learn something. Contraband "Love Potions" or "Sleeping Draughts" worked wonders on orcs. And that knowledge came in particularly handy then, especially when slipped into Red Dwarf dumplings. At least the gray-skinned goblin had been good for something.

I RACED THROUGH THE BUILDING. It was mostly dark and Morgan's flashlight became worth its weight in gold. I uttered a silent prayer to her, thanking her for being the kind of person who remembered to replace batteries, and also hoping she was okay. The elevator, like the Swift in my building, was out of order, and I had to run up what felt like eleventy thousand stairs to get to the top floor of the Winged Spire, where I knew the wizards held their seats. When I got there my knees were jelly and my lungs were on fire. I tried to tame my breathing as I approached. There were, of course, more orcs in security guard uniforms outside the door of the Council suite, and I was out of dumplings. There was only one thing to do. I walked up to them with my hands in the air.

As soon as they saw me, their fingers flew to their triggers. They furrowed their brows, looking me up and down, and I realized I was still wearing my Red Dwarf uniform under my coat. I buttoned it up, and they looked at me suspiciously.

"Egh?" said the one.

The other one frowned at me. "How did you get up here?"

I wished so hard right then for a quick and humble *impedio* spell. Nothing showy or complicated. All I needed was a moment so that I could get through the locked double doors they were guarding and approach one of the wizards inside.

"Get her out of here," the beefy orc said to his side-kick, who took a step toward me and lifted his AK47, aiming it at my chest. I was wearing my bulletproof coat, but those kinds of shells at point blank range would hurt like hell.

"Take her down to security."

"Wait," I said. "I have something they need," I gestured at the double-door, and the twitchier of the two almost blew my head off.

"What?"

My voice was shaky. "I'm going to reach into my pocket."

"No, you're not," said a voice from behind me. It was a human voice; even-toned and erudite. I spun on my heels. A man stood there. He had a long grey beard and was wearing the white robes edged with gold that I had only ever seen in photographs. He was a Council wizard.

I didn't know the correct etiquette. Was I supposed to bow, to curtsy? Even if I wanted to, I didn't know how. Instead I remained motionless.

"I'm Jacquel—," I said.

"I know who you are," said the wizard. "You'd better come in."

CHAPTER 25
CERBERUS

The wizard in the white robe lifted his staff and the doors unlocked then slid open, revealing a large, cozy room with a huge fire crackling in the hearth, and beautiful stained glass windows of stars and moons and planets. A couple of wizened faces looked up at us from where they were sitting.

I had expected a frantic energy; men rushing around, taking calls, helping people. But the Council wizards looked comfortably settled in their various chairs, reading animated newspapers and books, and watching the golden fire. They certainly didn't look too busy to eat dinner.

In fact, I saw not an anxious crease on their foreheads. That is, until they saw me.

A black-bearded wizard sitting near a window with a lead-outlined comet in its frame looked particularly unhappy to see me.

"You can't just walk in here," he said.

I wasn't sure how to respond to that. I had just literally walked in there. And breaking into the spire hadn't been too difficult, either.

"You need to upgrade your security," I said. "A couple of orcs in uniform is not enough."

"Clearly," said the man who had opened the doors for me.

"We've never needed high security," said Blackbeard. "Most people understand that one does not simply break into the Winged Spire. Any attempt on a Council wizard's life is punishable with immediate execution."

"Most people respect the laws of the Realm," said another wizard, standing up in what I thought was a threatening way.

"With all due respect," I said. "I tried calling. I tried hotlining. I tried to make an appointment but the receptionist said you're not seeing anyone."

"We're very busy," said Blackbeard, and the other wizards nodded and made sounds of agreement.

You don't look very busy, I thought, but I held my tongue. I had to remember that the Council had a collective wisdom beyond anything I could comprehend. If they were sitting around the fire reading books and newspapers and ignoring their dumplings then there must be a reason for it. I tried to remember my place, and be as polite as possible.

"I needed to see you urgently. I couldn't wait," I said. "I have something for you."

That seemed to pique their interest. I reached into my pocket and was stopped in my tracks by a deep growling sound. From the mat in front of the fire, a giant brown dog stood up and shook himself out. He was the size of a bear, and he had three heads.

I stared at him, too scared to move.

"It's all right," said the wizard behind me. He was standing a little too close for comfort, so I inched away. Was there a spark of menace in the room, or were my nerves just making me paranoid? Or maybe it was the supersized canine staring at me with his hungry yellow eyes. His jagged teeth reminded me of the werewolf chimera I had conjured as part of Bron's training. I had a feeling this hell hound wouldn't think twice about snapping me in half in one of his three salivating jaws. I looked at him, his copper tag swinging from his collar and catching the light of the fire. It flashed at me: one, two, three. The dog growled again, and I took a step back.

"What is it?" said Blackbeard. "What do you have for us?"

They all seemed to advance on me. It was gradual, almost imperceptible, but they were closing in.

All of a sudden I was thinking twice about handing over the Chaos Jar. I didn't feel safe, and I had to listen to my instinct, even though decades of common knowledge was telling me that the Council was, and had always been, ethically excellent and beyond reproach.

Don't forget they're the good guys, Morgan had said. *They're on our side.*

But my gut was disagreeing. My instinct was telling me to get the hell out of there. In fact, if my stomach was able to move independently from me, it would be hopping its way right out of that room.

"I have a question, first," I said.

"Have you forgotten where you are?" asked the wizard near the fire. "You don't get to break in here and then ask questions."

"I need to know why you planted a tail on me."

"We didn't plant a tail."

"Alif Farzad," I said, and there was a muted response. "You sent him to spy on me. Why?"

The men moved closer to me, and the three-headed dog followed suit. I stepped back. This hadn't worked out at all like I had hoped. I had—rather optimistically—expected an indifferent or annoyed response, followed by interest and thanks once I had handed over the Jar. But there was something in these wizards' eyes that I didn't like.

Yes, wizards—especially old male wizards—are known to be arrogant, and sometimes unfriendly, but this was different. The dog growled, a deep, resonant buzz, and moved his body in a way that scared me; as if he was preparing to pounce.

"That is Council business," said Blackbeard.

"I deserve to know," I said.

"You don't understand your place," said the man behind me, and I moved away from him again. He clearly didn't understand the concept of personal space, whereas I'm generally a big fan.

"What is it that you have for us?" said the wizard near the fire. He was wearing elven sneaking boots and there was no sound when he moved forward.

"Give it to us," said Blackbeard.

That was the final straw. There was no way I was handing over one of the elemental fragments to these psychos.

"Er," I said.

I had to give them something. I let go of the Jar and pulled out Zeel's notebook. Perfect.

"What's that?" said the man behind me.

It was the real thing, this time. I didn't have the conjuring magic to clone it.

"It's a comprehensive list of names and addresses of people who have been ordering contraband substances from EverShade."

"Impossible," said Blackbeard.

"Where did you get that?" said the other wizard, who was now standing in front of me.

"It's fake," said Blackbeard.

"It's not," I said, and handed it to him. He took the book and began turning the pages, frowning at what he was reading.

Maybe the book would make them realize that I was not the enemy. Maybe they'd see that I had the Realm's best interests at heart, handing in a book brimming with the names of their enemies. Hundreds of evil creatures could be rounded up, and the world would be a safer place.

Blackbeard closed the book and looked at me, danger glinting in his eyes.

"It's real," I said. "I swear on every planet in our solar system that book is real."

"I know it is," he said, and with a smooth arc of his arm, he threw the notebook into the fire. I watched it catch flame, saw the cover bubble as my heart climbed into my throat.

"Cerberus," he said to the dog. "Get her."

CHAPTER 26
THE MOST DANGEROUS PICKLE IN TOWN

The wizards watched as the dog, finally given permission to attack, launched himself at me. I wrenched the staff out of the wizard's hand—the white-robed man who had let me into the room—and I held it horizontally in front of me, saving myself from the animal's middle jaws as he crunched down on the wood. The other heads snarled and their saliva splashed onto me. I grabbed the staff back and ran, opening the doors and flying down the passage. Cerberus barked and chased after me. I was fit and strong, but the dog stayed at my heels, slowed only by his attempts to lock me in his jaws. I found an unmarked door and tried to open it, but it was locked. I kept running, Cerberus snapping at my boots. His paws slipped on the shiny tiles, giving me a slight advantage. Finally I found the fire escape door and launched myself at it, flinging it open, and then smashing it closed just as the dog caught up with me. It was just a matter of time before he splintered the wood or bent the bolt. I didn't wait to see that happen. I flung myself down the stairs and kept going till I reached the ground floor. The service entrance orcs were just waking up when I ran past them, groaning and rubbing their sweating stilton-cheese foreheads. I ran around the building, toward the parking lot where my Scorpion SUV was waiting for me. My cross-bow. My gun.

As soon as I caught sight of the car I clicked the button on the key to unlock it, and the lights flashed obediently. But as I lay my hands on the door handle, a huge meaty arm grabbed me from behind and lifted me into the air. I yelled and kicked, trying to break free. I was about to bite the bulging forearm when I saw a familiar car glide up. The handsome navy limousine I recognized from a previous life. I was carried to the car, and the back door opened smoothly.

Inside, splayed confidently on the luxurious cream leather seats, sat a pickle wearing lipstick. But it wasn't just any giant gherkin; it was one I knew very well. It was the most dangerous pickle in town.

"Hello, Jax," Shagar Khargol said.

I stopped fighting my abductor, and my body went limp. He dropped me. In slow motion, I climbed into the car, and he slammed the door shut after me.

"Drive," she said to the orc behind the smoked glass partition.

The limousine purred and sailed forward.

"Wait," I said. "I can't go with you. My things are back there. I need them."

"I'll bring you right back," she said. "We're just going to a little celebration."

"A celebration?"

"It'll all become clear to you soon."

"Let me just get my things," I said. "It'll only take a minute."

She glared at me; her eyes were wet clams. I gave up and sat back against the seat, resigning myself to the fact that I was under her thumb for the foreseeable future. I knew not to argue with Sugar. She had the breath of an alley rat, and a mean right hook.

"Keep your voice down," she said.

Why? I thought. *Who would hear us? Did she not trust her driver?*

Then I saw the baby strapped to her chest, and Sugar's lashes fluttered. I tried to think of something nice to say, but the truth was that orc babies were just as ugly as the grown versions. Not that I could see much of the tyke. She was flattened against Sugar's chest like a limpet, held in place by one of those special orc baby carriers that promised maximum pressure to simulate the uterus. A womb with a view.

I forced a smile. "She looks like you," I said, which seemed to make Shagar happy. At least it wasn't a lie. "I can't believe you came back."

"You asked me to," she said. "And you were right. I need to be here for my people. I need to stop Raguk Magra."

The fact that Hammerskins were killing Khargol children was made especially poignant now that there was an infant in the car.

"All the more reason for you to turn around and let me get my weapons."

"Oh, we don't have time for that," she said, patting the lump on her chest. "You'll be safe with us."

That I very much doubted, but in my position there was nothing much I could do. I'd have to go along on Shagar Khargol's unwelcome outing. She'd return me to my stolen cop car, and then I'd go looking for Morgan.

"Put your foot down!" she shouted at the driver. The engine roared, and we sped off.

"Are you going to tell me where we're going?" I asked.

She blinked at me, then checked her lipstick in a small mirror she pulled from her handbag.

"Let's keep it a surprise, shall we?"

CHAPTER 27
A PUNCH BOWL AND A PIÑATA

There was only one reason Shagar Khargol would want to keep our destination a surprise, and it wasn't because there was a punch bowl and a piñata waiting for us. Wherever she was taking me, she knew that I wouldn't agree to go if she was upfront about it.

"Thanks for the fruit basket," I said.

She smiled at me, showing her mossy tombstone teeth in all their rotten glory. The baby began to get restless. She was snorting and mewling, and it reminded me of holding Samantha Farzad's newborn. Shagar unclipped the harness. The baby, sensing the warm solid flesh she had lost, began to cry at full volume. Shagar held the shrieking baby in one hand and pulled down the top of her dress with the other, exposing a breast swollen with milk. I looked out of the tinted window while Sugar plugged the baby's wide open mouth with her purple nipple. There was a loud suckling noise and the baby's tiny hands held fast onto Shagar's skin.

The limousine was racing through the city streets, but it felt as if my mind was sprinting faster. I ignored the signs of devastation beyond the glass. The burning houses and dead bodies. The animals lining the streets, the people possessed by the plague. What had become of this place?

I tried to switch myself off from what I was seeing and instead attempted to make sense of what had happened at the spire. My insides were simmering with fear and dread, and also a kind of sorrow that I was surprised by. I suppose I had always thought of the Council as a kind of band of fathers who looked after everyone in the Realm. They protected us, they always knew best, they were quick with discipline. In my mind, the Council kept the world spinning. Perhaps the feeling was stronger for me than it was for others, as I'd lost my father so young. At least I had the Council looking after me, I thought. But why have they turned on me? They burnt Zeel's notebook of dark arts practitioners; they set their guard dog on me. What can I say? Discovering that your father wants you dead is a pretty shattering experience. No matter how much I tried to untangle the threads, I couldn't make sense of it.

"I'm going to need your help," said Shagar.

"I guessed as much," I said. "I'm sorry to disappoint you, but I'm not able to sling spells at the moment."

Or maybe ever.

I showed her my volt cuff, and looking at the vile thing again made me wonder why Musubarin had not yet electrocuted me. What was he waiting for?

"That's a shame," she said, sniffing. "But it's only a minor setback."

"Speak for yourself," I said. My life had never been a very neat affair, but in the last couple of days it had been turned upside down and inside out. And not in a good way.

Sugar set her jaw and plucked the baby off her breast, burped her, then settled her onto the other side. "You won't need your magic for this particular occasion."

"Easy for you to say. I'm used to using magic for everything. I feel completely useless, now. Especially knowing that we're going somewhere dangerous."

Our gazes met, and she shrugged. "Yes," she said. "I guess you could say that."

AROUND TEN MINUTES LATER, the car began to slow, but it was so dark outside I found it difficult to tell where we were. But then I saw the fortress, and the flag. My blood turned to ice water.

"No-o-o-o," I exhaled. "No, Shagar, no. This is a bad idea." I was shaking my head, tapping my feet. "Let me out."

I tried to open the door, but of course it was locked. I would have known that if I could think straight, but my nerves were short-circuiting my brain.

"Let me out," I said again.

Sugar ignored me. She burped the baby one last time and handed her to me.

"No!" I said. "What are you doing?"

"Take the baby," said Sugar, her voice as smooth and cold as orc steel.

"No!" I said again. I was not taking her baby. I was not going into the fortress with her. I was not dying that night.

We approached the gate, and six Hammerskins armed to the hilt stepped forward. I looked past them, up at the fortress, and my fingers tingled with fright. Usually I'd expect some sparks to gather in my hands, but there was nothing. I felt like weeping. I felt like running away.

The flag whipped around in the wind, making a snapping sound.

Had Sugar gone mad? Had her jaunt at the Khargol Isles made her soft in the head? Why on earth would she choose to come here? To walk right into the lion's den?

And this was no ordinary lion. This was a black-maned beast, a scarred animal with no empathy or respect for anyone but his own ego. His thirst for power had killed more people in the past few days than had died in the third Realm war in '79.

We were his sworn enemies, and we had just delivered ourselves, in a fancy limousine, to our own deaths.

CHAPTER 28
ALCAZAR

I stared at Shagar Khargol. She would have a hell of a lot of explaining to do when we arrived in Halloween Heaven.

"Take the baby," she said again, and I took it. She passed me the baby carrier, too, and a small vial of potion. I blinked at her, then swallowed it in one gulp. It tasted of mud and sparks.

Almost immediately, my lips began to swell, and then my hands, as if I was having some kind of allergic reaction. I watched as my body inflated like a jumping castle. My eyes bulged, my stomach snapped my belt, and my mouth turned into a cemetery.

Shagar looked at me with approval, and I quickly strapped the sleeping baby to my chest.

She placed one of her manicured frankfurters on the window button, and pressed it so that the glass slid all the way down. The Hammerskin peering in took a step back and clutched his weapon, a giant automatic rifle that he wore slung from his shoulder. He trained it on Shagar.

"Ergh?" he said.

Another orc stepped up, and looked just as confused. They hadn't received the memo, either, that their prime enemy was coming for tea. Within seconds, we had half a dozen weapons pointing at our heads.

"Tell Magra I am here," said Shagar in her most royal accent.

The orcs blinked at us, then one of them slowly lowered his rifle and grabbed the walkie-talkie off his belt. He spoke in a strange dialect that I didn't understand, and the conversation went back and forth a little, until he finally shrugged and replaced the radio. He instructed the other men to stand down, and the heavy black gate shuddered open.

"Drive slowly," said the man, and all six of the guards walked alongside the limo as we drove up the black path toward the towering fortress. I had seen pictures of the Hammerskin citadel on the news, but none of those photos had done it justice. Alcazar was a huge, imposing building, an old wreck from the days of war, rebuilt and fortified by the Neo-Nazis rendering it completely impenetrable from the outside. The scene was monochromatic: the building appeared lit up, faded and patchwork gray against the dark sky. The security floodlights were huge and unforgiving. The men marched alongside us and I felt like a prisoner heading to the guillotine. It made me wonder why everyone seemed so damned intent on getting me killed.

The limousine rolled to a stop, and the men opened our doors for us. When the driver tried to get out, they shoved a gun in his face and told him he could wait in the car. He lifted his hands in surrender. Sugar climbed out of the car, as did I.

I felt intensely uncomfortable in my orc glamour get-up. I made sure the baby was secure against my chest and prayed that Sugar had a plan. I had to remind myself that Shagar Khargol, despite her looks, was one of the smartest, deadliest people I knew. As we walked forward, toward the huge fortress gates, I hoped she would live up to my estimation of her.

THE GATES UNLOCKED WITH A LOUD, thudding clunk, and we entered. There were Hammerskins everywhere. Every post, every doorway, every window, and they all had their guns pointing in our direction.

"One false move," whispered Shagar to me, "and we'll be fed to the crocodiles."

I couldn't tell if she was joking or not. I swallowed hard and looked at her. There were no crocodiles in the city, were there? Still, I took her point, and moved slowly and carefully. The last thing I needed was to trip over something and foil the magnificent plan I was hoping Shagar had.

We were marched through the cobbled square, under the persistent flapping and snapping of the flag, and into the core of the fortress. Weapons regarded us at every turn. The baby squirmed against me, so I patted her back and swayed her a bit, and she fell back asleep. It was such an odd sensation to comfort a baby, as if my body automatically knew what to do. I had always assumed I'd be clueless when it came to looking after a child, but my hips swayed almost of their own accord. Muscle memory, maybe, from a previous life. Or an inbuilt instinct to nurture that I'd never given a chance to surface. There's not much time to learn baby sign-language when you're knocking off vampires for a living.

As we walked through Alcazar I wondered what it would be like to hang up my crossbow and have a little Darick Junior crawling around my haunted apartment. Ghost could wash and iron his little miniature socks and onesies, and I'd order in healthy dinners. We'd eat in the jungle kitchen amongst the golden gibbons. Gizmo would have a place at the table, and so would Bron. The doorbell would ring, and I'd jump up to answer it, ready to greet Darick with a rib-cracking hug, Ferra Fernak style.

But in my daydream, when I opened the door, it wasn't Darick standing there, but Lysander, polished fangs bright against the night. And he swept in and kissed Darick Junior on the head, and then I saw with horror that my baby wasn't a dark-haired Darick Junior at all, but a blond Lysander Junior.

My heart was hammering.

No, no, I told myself. *That's not how it goes.*

I tried again. Instead of giving into my anxiety I funneled it into another nonsense fantasy. This time, Darick would be the one ringing the doorbell. I stood up from the kitchen table and walked to the door. Darick, I told myself. Darick's behind the door. It's my daydream, and I'm deciding that Darick is behind the door. But when I opened it, Musubarin stood there. He snapped his fingers and handcuffs appeared on my wrists. I shouted out and spun round to look at my baby, but the plant had eaten the table and everyone at it, and only a jungle remained.

I tried one more time to force my brain to cooperate. Darick behind the door, I told myself. No one but Darick. This time, when I opened the door, it was Darick. Joy! I was about to fling myself at him when I registered the shocked grimace on his face. What? I thought. Did I have spinach in my teeth? And then I looked down at my body, and it was an orc body. The potion wasn't a glamour at all, but a permanent potion that rendered my skin into blue cheese, my teeth into decaying planks. A rotten white picket fence.

Deodamnatus, I thought. My fear was running through every part of me. I was so far gone I couldn't even imagine a happy ending to a daydream. It was not a good sign.

FINALLY WE APPROACHED another set of giant doors, made of solid timber, bolts, and big black hinges. The fortress had a medieval feel to it, which added to my sense of dread. The doors creaked as our chaperones showed us in.

Raguk Magra was alone in the cavernous room. It was made of stone, and freezing inside. Water dripped some-where out of sight, and I could hear the shuffling of the guards outside the doors they had just closed. The massive fireplace was clean and cold. He dragged his eyes away from whatever it was that he was looking at outside and regarded us politely. He didn't look like a coldblooded killer, but, in my experience, they seldom did.

"Raguk," said Shagar. "It's been a long time."

I blinked so hard at hearing that, it felt like I had devel-oped a tic in my left eye.

Raguk Magra strode toward us, and Shagar went all coy, and curtsied. When I didn't follow suit, she elbowed me in the side.

"You look well," Magra said. "You haven't aged a bit. And is that a ... tan, I see?"

Sugar made a snorting sound. It could have been a laugh, but I wouldn't put money on it.

"You are the one who looks well," she said. "Power suits you."

Then it was Magra's turn to snort. I guess you could say he was handsome—for an orc—but that would be like saying a skunk was sweet-smelling, for a skunk. Or that a hunter was gentle, for a hunter. None of which really made sense. Perhaps it was better to say that Raguk Magra was one of the least ugly orcs I had met. And he seemed to like the look of Shagar, too, judging by the way he hadn't taken his eyes off her since the moment she swept into the room.

"You've come at a good time," he said, swishing his robe. "We've had a successful week. I was about to reward the men with a midnight feast. Please, join us."

"We'd love to," Shagar said, which made Raguk's eyes dance with light. "But, first, I'd like to talk. It won't take long."

Magra nodded. "As you wish, my lady."

CHAPTER 29
ORC BLOOD

One of Raguk Magra's men brought us drinks on a tarnished silver tray: a snifter of orc brandy for him, and dry sherry for Sugar and I. Sugar took a glass for herself but shooed mine away. I had been introduced as the baby's wet nurse, and I had to play the part. Also, as per Copperfield Institute Potions 101, you shouldn't mix booze with magic. In such esteemed company, I couldn't risk my glamour fading. I watched as they took my triple shot away, and I couldn't say I wasn't sorry. The alcohol would have dampened the anxiety I felt barbing my stomach, and stopped my hands from trembling.

Shagar rose from the scrubbed table and walked over to the neglected fireplace. It was like a huge mouth, dark and with blackened metal teeth, hungry for fire. Sugar got down on her knees and began to lay the kindling, then some branches. She broke a fire-lighter in two and placed them carefully inside the structure, lit them, then added some hunks of wood to the top. When she seemed happy that the fire had taken, she stood up, dusted her hands and wiped the soot from her knees. We watched as the flames leapt and licked the grain of the wood and the kindling crackled and curled. The fire immediately added warmth to the room. It wasn't just the change in temperature, but the soft light and the smell of burning timber that transformed the space from gray and cold to warm and cozy.

Gezudlick, as Ferra would have said.

Raguk had watched the ritual in silence, and seemed pleased. When Sugar sat back down with us, she put her hands on the table between her and Magra and gave him an intense look. I was sure that Magra could see the flames reflected in her eyes.

"I am here to ask you an important question," said Shagar.

Raguk Magra took a long sip of his brandy. "Go ahead."

"I find myself in a vulnerable position," she said. "And I don't like feeling vulnerable."

Magra nodded.

"My husband is dead," she said. "I have a child to look after. And my people—"

"Indeed," he said. "The Khargol familia is not in a good position."

I couldn't help picturing the slaughter. Men, women, children. It was difficult to conceive that this man across the table, this least-ugly orc with impeccable manners, was responsible for such wholesale bloodshed.

"Raguk. I think there is a deal to be made."

He blinked at her, as if he hadn't heard correctly. "A deal?" he said. "Between the Khargols and the Hammerskins? That would be..."

"That would be the answer to your dilemma, and mine," she said.

"Dilemma?" he demanded. "I have no dilemma. I am winning the war." Then he stopped and held up a bratwurst finger. "I have *won* the war."

"You think you have won the war," said Sugar. "But I still have thousands of men. I have an army ready to fight and die for the Khargol name. Your army is strong, Raguk, but the Khargol loyalists outnumber your forces a hundred to one."

I could see the muscles in his jaw moving as he ground his teeth. He knew she was right. It had been optimistic of him to think that they had all fled the Realm.

"On the surface it looks like the Hammerskins have seized power, but that's just because my men have been driven underground. They're preparing for the final battle. They're armed, and waiting."

"Waiting?" he said. "Waiting for what?"

She spent a moment looking at him, then took her phone out of her handbag and laid it, face-down, on the table. "For my command."

Raguk downed his brandy and then slammed the empty glass down, narrowing his eyes at Shagar. His servant hurried up to the table and refilled it.

He scratched his beard. "How do I know you're telling the truth?"

"You already know it's the truth," she said, sliding her hands a little closer to him.

"What are you waiting for, then? Why not give the command right now?"

"Because I have a better plan," she said, and her eyes twinkled with orange flames.

Shagar Khargol stood up and moved towards the fire.

"It's a dangerous time," she said. "The Realm is unstable. The city is in havoc. The untouched humans are behaving in a troubling way. It appears that there is wild magic at play."

"Yes," he said.

My cheeks burned.

"The last thing the Realm needs is another great war. Even if the Khargols win—which I'm confident we'll do—what will there be left to govern? What will be left of our economy? Civilians of ravaged countries do not pay tax. Injured and desperate people require assistance. After the war, whoever's in power will be besieged with problems. There'll be no payoff with a stalled economy."

Raguk tapped his fingertips on the table.

"I'd be inheriting problems, not power. And I'm not interested in that. I won't preside over a battle just for the sake of the win. There are easier ways to inflate one's ego."

He gazed at her in that intense way again. "So what is your question?" he asked. "You said you had a question."

"I'll get to that," she said. "First, there is the issue of the Silvano Clan."

Raguk threw the brandy down his throat again and gestured for more.

"I know about your deal with them, Magra. Which is bad news for both of us. Because even if you wanted to call off our feud, you can't. You've promised the Silvanos a victory."

He lowered his eyes to the table and scratched at the wood. "I did what I had to do."

"If anyone else," said Shagar. "If any other orc had made a deal with vampires—a deal with the devil—I would have called him a stupid, disloyal bastard. But I know you, Raguk."

He looked at her again.

"I know you, Raguk," she said again. "And you are none of those things. But you have painted yourself into a corner with those bloodsuckers. Now you're going to have to fight or die."

"Fight or die," he said.

"I don't want you to die. I don't want your men to die."

Magra's eyes were glowing coals. Sugar's words hung in the air. She clenched her hands into fists and slammed them on the table.

"Because orc blood runs in my veins. Not Khargol blood. Not Hammerskin blood. Orc blood. The last thing I want is to see our people—" she flattened her hands out again and lowered her voice. "*Our people* destroyed by a war no one can really win."

Magra was brooding. He knew she was right, but it was an impossible position to be in.

"Why are you here, Shagar?"

"I'm here to offer you a way out."

CHAPTER 30
VELOUR BRUT

"Why, after all the work you've put into this *coup*, should you hand the power over to vampires?"

"Because that was the deal," Raguk said. "I help them seize power of the Realm, and they will ensure I keep my position, amongst some other ... perks."

Sugar's baby began to fuss, so I rocked her a bit and patted her back. It seemed to break Sugar's concentration, but not for long. She turned her body to face Raguk.

"You've made a deal with the Silvano clan, but that doesn't mean you need to honor it."

He grunted. "If I don't honor it I'll die an ugly death."

And so you should, I caught myself thinking. He didn't

deserve a way out. He deserved to have his decapitated head on a spike.

"I think there is a new deal to be made," she said.

Raguk cocked his head and looked at her. "I'm listening."

She glanced pointedly at her phone, which was still laying face-down on the table. "I call my men and tell them to stand down. They'll disarm and defuse the bombs—"

"Bombs?" said Raguk. "You didn't say anything about bombs."

"For years we've had access to an underground military bunker," said Sugar. "Left over from the last war. Forgotten by authorities."

The way she said *forgotten* made me think that some money had crossed hands in order for those particular memories to be consigned to oblivion.

"You wouldn't believe the weapons we found in there," she said, "but let's not get distracted by the details. My men will stand down;the bombs will be defused."

"A truce," said Magra.

"Better than a truce," she said. "Because with our combined forces, we'll be stronger than the enemy."

Magra grunted in what I thought sounded like approval.

"Raguk," she said. "Raguk." She had a way of saying his name so that it sounded like the title of a romantic hero, instead of a monkey retching. "Do you understand what I am saying? If we join forces, we can defeat the Silvanos, and any other vampires that stand in our way."

He was nodding very slightly, perhaps thinking of what it would be like to get rid of the vampires for good, and to rule the Realm with a fellow pickle-face who he clearly found attractive.

He cleared his throat. "It's a good plan," he admitted.

"It's the only plan," Shagar said. "If you want to stay alive."

Raguk would get exactly what he had been scheming for. Plus he would get to live. It seemed like a definite win-win.

Shagar stepped up to him and offered her baseball mitt of a hand to shake. "Deal?"

Magra took a moment, then stood up and shook her hand. In a gruff voice, he agreed. They had a deal. There was palpable relief in the room. I felt like I had been holding my breath for their entire conversation.

"AND NOW, FOR MY QUESTION," said Shagar. She pulled her eyes away from Raguk and looked at me. "Nurse," she said, sweetly. "Please go to the car and get the gifts from the trunk. Take your time."

I stared at her, confused, but not wanting to give anything away. "Yes ma'am," I said.

Raguk, with a knowing expression, told his servant to accompany me, to help carry. They wanted privacy, and I was desperate to know why. I trudged out of the room and walked with the orcs through the fortress passages and out to the limousine. When the driver and security guard saw me coming, they opened their doors and climbed out, and clicked the trunk open without me having to say anything. As the lid sprang open, I flinched. I couldn't help it. In my job you get used to nasty surprises. Would it be a dead body? A load of dynamite? A goblin with an AK47?

But I needn't have worried, because when I looked into the recess all I saw were champagne bottles—hundreds of them, neatly packed in boxes with raffia—and a huge bouquet of white flowers. How did Sugar know about the midnight victory feast in Alcazar? I pulled a bottle out and looked at the label. It was the real deal. Velour Brut, from a well-known Elven wine estate. Not the cheap sweet sparkling stuff you get down in the SubRealm on New Year's Eve. These orcs wouldn't know what hit them. The driver and the bodyguard loaded up some boxes, as did Raguk's servant, and I carried the enormous bouquet of flowers and the small red suitcase embossed with gold initials: SK.

. . .

WE ARRIVED BACK at the room and knocked politely on the door. After a few moments, Shagar answered. She had soot on her knees again, and her lipstick was smudged.

Oh, I thought. *That's why she wanted some privacy.*

But then she said something that made my head spin.

"Nurse," she said. "You can be the first to congratulate us."

"Er—" I said.

"Champagne!" said Raguk, who suddenly seemed to be in an excessively chipper mood.

I hauled the flowers up and onto the table, and Sugar took the suitcase from me.

"Congratulate you on what?" I asked. But then I looked around at the bubbly and the flowers, and Sugar opened her case and took out an XXXL tuxedo, and a white lace dress.

"There's going to be a wedding," Raguk said. "First wedding in the fortress."

I stared at Sugar, and she looked rather breathless. "We're getting married," she said.

CHAPTER 31
TOAST

As the midnight feast had already been prepared, all that needed to be done was to put the champagne on ice and call the lapsed evangelical orc pastor to preside over the ceremony. I helped Shagar into her wedding dress, which was two sizes too small—the woman had practically just given birth, after all—while two of the female Hammerskins stood with their backs to the walls, silently watching us, and no doubt listening to every word we said. I did my best with her hair and make-up, but I couldn't help feeling it was a little like trying to decorate a cucumber, which was a losing battle if I ever fought one. Still, I dabbed some foundation powder over her Stiltonesque skin and lined her greasy eyelids with a kohl pencil.

"You look beautiful," I lied. I still felt awkward in my orc body, and knew I wasn't much to look at, either. Orc glamours certainly have a way of keeping you humble. I hoped the effects of the potion would last long enough to get me through the wedding or it would certainly raise some eyebrows. Shagar quickly gave the baby some milk behind a screen, then handed her back to me.

"Take care of her," she said, with a pointed expression.

"Of course," I said, strapping the infant to my chest. But then a panicky feeling crawled up my throat.

Take care of her? Like, take care of her while I'm marrying a murderous dictator, or take care of her forever because I'm not making it out of here alive tonight?

"Sugar?" I said.

"It's time," said one of our Neo-Nazi attendants, ending our rather short conversation. We nodded and followed the women out of the guest room and through the narrow stone corridors. After a few minutes the passage opened up to reveal a huge hall decorated with posters of Raguk, and toilet paper bunting.

"It was the best I could do at such late notice," he said, and we both looked up at him. He looked perfectly dapper in the tuxedo. It was beautifully cut, as if it had been made for him. He took Sugar's banana-fingered hands in his own. "You look stunning," he said, his voice gruff.

What was grating his voice? Desire? Happiness? Fear? I wasn't sure.

Two long tables took up the floor space, and there was a makeshift dance floor in the corner. The tables groaned under platters of food. Baskets of fresh fruit, pans of roasted meats still steaming. The aroma of freshly baked bread rolls reached me, and the werewolf in my stomach growled.

The soon-to-be-married couple's table was adjacent to the other two, and elevated, and their chairs were thrones. They took their seats and watched as the Hammerskins began to stream in from the entrance below. Once the orcs had taken their seats, Raguk and Shagar stood up, and Raguk called for silence.

The pastor began his sermon, but halfway through his second sentence Raguk interrupted him.

"Skip to the important bit," he commanded.

The man nodded nervously, then put his notes back in his pocket.

"Do you, Shagar Khargol, take this man, Raguk Magra, to be your lawfully wedded husband?"

Sugar turned to Raguk and took his hands in hers. "I do," she said. They didn't break eye contact.

"And do you, Raguk Magra, take this woman, Shagar Khargol, as your lawfully wedded wife?"

"I do," said Magra, and they both smiled.

"Then, by the powers vested in me by the Realm, I now pronounce you man and wife."

The newlywed couple leaned into a kiss that was so filled with lust that I had to look away. If anyone doubted the potential success of the marriage, that kiss may have certainly convinced them. There was a moment of silence from the Hammerskins, and I worried that they'd reject the union, but then there was a roar of applause, whistling and cheering, and I realized Magra had informed his men of the benefits the marriage would bring them. Combined forces. More men, more artillery.

Of course, convincing the victimized Khargols might be a bit trickier, I thought, *but that was a problem for another day.*

The newly-minted Magras unlocked their lips for long enough to call for champagne, and the crowd whooped and cheered again. Shagar's baby was woken by the noise, so I shushed her and rocked her, and she settled down.

Still standing, Magra called for a toast. Champagne corks popped and glasses chinked. Everyone in the giant hall stood and filled their flutes, cups, and goblets. Shagar and Raguk had their own bottle of brut with a bespoke label on it, an illustration of a heart with an arrow through it, their initials nestling inside. Raguk wrenched the bottle out of the ice and twisted the gold wire open, then he eased the cork out with his thick thumbs. It opened with a bang and a fizz and bubbles cascaded out. Shagar giggled and held the flutes out, and her new husband poured them each a glass.

"A toast!" yelled Magra. "To my beautiful wife."

The orcs cheers and wolf-whistled, making Shagar blush and bat her eyelashes.

"To a brighter future," he said, and there was more cheering. "And to victory!" He took Shagar's hand and held it up in the air, as if they had just won a race.

"Victory!" They all shouted "Victory! Victory!"

Raguk laughed and held the glass to his lips.

"Stop!" shouted someone. "Stop! Don't drink that!"

And we all stopped, dead in our tracks. The Hammerskin commander general stepped forward, the medals on his green military uniform flashing. "Put your drinks down," he said, and everyone obeyed. They looked around uncertainly.

"General," said Raguk. "What is the meaning of this?"

"Indulge me, sir. Just for a moment."

Raguk looked supremely annoyed. His anger bloomed on his skin, turning it red at his collar as the blush crept up towards his face. "What are you doing?" he asked the general.

"My job."

He looked at Shagar. "Mrs. Khargol," he said.

"Mrs. Magra," she corrected him.

"Mrs. Magra," he said. "Please, go ahead. Have a sip of your champagne."

Shagar frowned at him. "What?"

"Have a sip," he said.

"Look here, General," said Raguk, pawing at the irritated skin on his neck. "I won't have you talking to my wife—"

"No, it's all right," said Sugar, putting a hand on Raguk's arm. "It's all right. He's a good man. A good general."

She lifted her glass, moved her head back, and tipped the entire contents of the flute down her throat. Then she straightened up and looked at the general and smiled. The room waited with bated breath.

Suddenly Sugar began to look uncomfortable. Her throat wobbled, and she crimped her lips shut.

Oh holy faex, I thought, eyeing the closest exit. If Shagar keeled over I'd have to sprint out of here.

She started blinking, and her eyes began to water. Her hand crept up to her chest.

Filius canis, I thought. I took a deep breath and readied my muscles to run.

Then Sugar stunned the crowd by letting out the mother of all belches. It was a roar of a burp, and I could swear I saw the flowers on the table wilt in its aftermath.

Then she covered her mouth coyly, and smiled. "I beg your pardon," she said, and the men roared with laughter. The general nodded, did a half-bow, and stood down. If anything, the moment had won the army over, and there was a happiness in the hall that had been missing earlier, through the cheering and whistling.

The couple sat down on their thrones and laughed. They both looked relieved, and I watched as the Hammerskins all around me start gulping down their expensive elf champagne and tearing into the roasted birds and bread rolls.

CHAPTER 32
CLAIMING VICTORY

Raguk tipped his champagne into this mouth, too, and the couple kissed again, and I watched as Sugar's hand traveled down Raguk's chest and stomach, and disappeared beneath the table. His expression softened, and I saw his eyes melt with desire. With her other hand, she pulled him by his lapel toward her, and whispered something in his ear. I could see that his neck was still red from before, and he unbuttoned his collar to attempt to relieve it. Shagar finished whispering and Raguk looked at her with a wolfish grin.

Holding hands, they left the table, and disappeared behind an old, faded velvet curtain. I stood up. I had to follow them. I had to find out what was going on, plus I was starting to feel the beginning of the glamour potion fading, and I couldn't be in the company of drunk Hammerskins when that happened.

As I was slipping away, one of the orcs grabbed me and tried to kiss me. I had to stop myself from going full-on kamikaze and chopping him in the throat with my forearm. I reminded myself to stay in character. To act like a wet nurse, not a wizard who knew her way around an attacker. So instead of kicking him in the toolbox, I gestured at the baby strapped to my chest—a detail he had missed when he had lunged at me—and he put his hand up and backed off, allowing me to disappear behind the purple curtain.

I followed the trail of champagne-scented orc breath down a dark stone passage, and up a flight of stairs. The interior of the fortress was deserted. Every guard, servant and general dogsbody was in the great hall, celebrating the union of the orc tribes. Still, I climbed up the gray steps quietly. I couldn't afford to be caught. As I watched my feet land on the stairs, I saw them shrinking down to regular human size, and my belly deflated, my legs thinned out. All of a sudden I had a neck again, and my cheeks weren't wheels of brie. A quick sweep of my tongue across my teeth revealed that my mouth had also returned to normal. Physically, it was a relief to be back in my normal body, but I also knew I was in a heap of trouble. If anyone saw me then, Shagar and I would have a lot of explaining to do.

I crept up the stairs, right to the top where the room opened up. I followed the giggling I guessed could only be coming from Sugar, and approached yet another passage, and then the main bedroom. I held my breath and flattened myself against the flagstone wall, and peered in. A screen of billowing voile curtain separated me from the married couple, so I could just barely see their shapes against the light of the fire in the hearth. I noticed it was pre-lit this time, and didn't require Shagar to go down on her knees for the third time that night. Although, judging by the sounds coming from the couple, you never could tell.

"Don't take it off," said Sugar. "The tuxedo. You look so handsome I could just eat you up."

Raguk groaned. There was some kissing, some muttering. Then a squelching sound that made me want to pour acid in my ears.

"I'll fire the general in the morning," Raguk said.

"Don't," she said. "He was just trying to protect you. He's a good man."

"He's not a good man," Raguk said. "Not a good man."

"Why?" said Shagar, panting. I could hear her bracelets jingling.

"He's too ruthless," Raguk said.

"That's rich, coming from you."

"I mean it. He's the one who ordered the killing of insurgents. All of them. It's been his plan from the beginning, and I let him go too far."

I heard some slapping sounds, which I tried to ignore. I couldn't even think about the rainbows and puppies, because they were tainted by the images I had of the HobNob Olympics.

"Let him drink some of that champagne," said Shagar. "It might loosen him up."

Raguk laughed. He was out of breath. "The general doesn't drink alcohol. He never lets his guard down."

Shagar was puffing and panting then, and it sounded like she was about to erupt. "Can we stop talking about the general? All I want is you. Look at me, Raguk."

Magra let out a long groan.

"Look at me, Raguk," she said again. "I want you to look at me when I claim victory."

Magra groaned again, and Shagar joined in, until their voices hit a crescendo together.

Calling that particular exchange *claiming a victory* was an odd turn of phrase, I thought, but to each their own. Who was I to judge?

Then there was another kind of grunt, more like a gurgle, and a thump as a large body hit the ground. I drew the curtain aside. The great Raguk Magra lay dead on the floor.

Shagar, naked apart from a pair of blue suspenders, looked up at me. "Good," she said. "You're here."

CHAPTER 33
STRAIGHT TO THE HEART

The ruthless leader of the Hammerskin Tribe lay dead, clothed from the waist up in the tuxedo Sugar had given him. Everywhere the fabric touched him was purple and blotchy, with small blisters. I remembered the night I was traversing the EverShade market. One of the items for sale was poisoned underwear. Shagar had done one better: a poisoned wedding tuxedo.

"I don't know whether to be impressed by you," I whispered. "Or very scared."

Shagar smiled at me, but didn't answer. She ripped the rest of Raguk's suit off and threw it into the fire, then pulled on her too-tight wedding dress. "We need to get out of here," she said, "before the general finds us."

I couldn't stop looking at Raguk's torso, veined with purple and covered with the red rash the magical toxin had caused. Shagar caught me staring.

"If you lace the shirt in the chest area the poison goes straight to the heart."

I nodded, but I couldn't think of an appropriate response.

You should start a blog, I thought, *101 Hacks for Husband-Killers.*

"Help me," she said. "We need to move the body."

I looked around. "Where?"

Magra was a huge orc and probably weighed around the same as a great white shark. I had a sleeping baby strapped to my chest and the Chaos Jar in my pocket.

"There's a trapdoor in the next room," she said.

That's when I realized that Sugar Shagar left nothing to chance. She had studied the blueprint for Alcazar. She seemed brazen, but really was cold and calculated.

Raguk's head reverberated off the uneven floor as we dragged the body across the flagstone passage and into the adjoining room. I didn't see a trapdoor, but Shagar blinked a few times, looking around the room to orientate herself, then pointed at the four-poster bed. We scraped it across the floor and lifted the rug below, revealing the trapdoor.

THE CHAOS JAR

Shagar opened it, and the air that escaped was cold and musty.

"What's down there?" I asked, with a shiver, but Shagar didn't answer. We puffed and panted, getting Raguk's bulk to the square hole in the floor and pushed him through it. He landed with thump and a crack, which I was pretty sure was his skull fracturing. I couldn't help grimacing.

"Don't feel bad for him," said Sugar. It sounded like an order.

I looked up at her. There wasn't a trace of empathy or guilt in her eyes.

"He colluded with vampires for power. He killed my people," she said. "He killed children."

I slammed the trapdoor closed and dusted my hands. We moved the rug and bed back into place and began striding back to the limousine.

"You thought of everything," I said.

"No," Sugar said, lips pursed. "I didn't know that the general doesn't drink."

I didn't understand what she meant by that, but soon it became clear. When we moved past the great hall we weren't greeted by the drunken singing and revelry I had expected. Instead there was an eerie silence. I frowned at

Shagar, trying to work it out, when we stuck our heads in to have a look.

The tables and floors were covered with dead bodies. The Hammerskins lay all over each other, eyes bulging, violet tongues swollen and protruding. I had seen that look before. A champagne cork rolled toward me, and I picked it up. At the base of the mushroom shape was just the merest hint of purple.

"Indigo Violent?" I asked her, and she nodded.

Seeing so many dead bodies was a shock to me. There must have been two hundred men there, most of Raguk's army. Sure, there would still be a few Neo-Nazi orcs in the city, holding fort, but most of them were here, lying dead on the floor. And all at the hand of the woman who stood beside me. She had also been surveying the hall, and our eyes met at the same time. She looked at my chest, where her baby was strapped tightly.

"She's going to need some milk," Sugar said. "I'll feed her in the car."

She handed me a key from her handbag.

When I looked at her, puzzled, she said: "Spare key. You drive."

"Me?" I said.

What about your driver? I was going to ask, but then I saw both the driver and the bodyguard lying dead amongst the Hammerskins.

"Sacrifices have to be made," she said.

If the Khargol men had not partaken of the champagne, the enemy would have been suspicious. I took a deep breath.

"Okay," I said. "I'll drive."

CHAPTER 34
SOMETIMES KARMA IS A REAL FILIUS CANIS

Sometimes Karma is a Real Filius Canis

We were silent on the drive back to the Winged Spire parking lot to get my SUV. I was still in shock. I heard the baby suckle and gurgle and was comforted by the sounds. Of course it was a huge relief that the Hammerskin problem was mostly solved, but now we'd have the general to contend with. He was the ruthless one, Raguk had said. Remembering his words made me feel chilled and empty inside. I had missed out on the dinner at the victory feast, so I unwrapped one of Morgan's protein bars and scarfed it down. My mouth was too dry, and it got stuck in my throat.

When we arrived at the Council building parking lot, the SUV was gone.

At first I couldn't believe it, and I thought I had parked it somewhere else. I kept looking for it, but it was gone. The car I had stolen had been stolen. Sometimes Karma is a real *filius canis.*

My crossbow was gone. Panic swept over me, followed by an intense hopelessness.

I turned off the limo engine and lowered my forehead to the steering wheel. I rested it there for a full minute. Not only was my magic gone, but I had lost my ride and my weapons. I took my phone out of my pocket and checked the signal. Nothing. How would I be able to find Morgan? How could I check on Ferra? Walking around anywhere in the city then, unarmed, would be a suicide mission.

"Faex," I muttered. *"Faex!"*

I felt like slamming my fist into the steering wheel, but broken knuckles would just add to my 99 problems. Instead, I began to cry, and I hated myself for it.

"You can come stay at the bunker tonight," said Sugar. "I need to see some people, but Gnarg is there. He'll protect you. It's safe."

The tears kept flowing. My body and mind were exhausted. I kept picturing Magra's blistered torso, and hearing the sound of his body hitting the floor, his skull cracking. Kept seeing the keeled-over wedding guests overlaid with the pictures of the Khargol loyalists' heads on spikes.

Too much violence. Too much death.

"Start the car," she said. "I'll direct you."

"No," I said, shaking my head. I swiped the tears away and took a deep breath to steady myself. "No. No hiding in bunkers. I have things to do."

People to find.

"All right," she said. She burped the baby and strapped it to her chest, then climbed out of the car and took the keys from me. She gestured to the passenger seat, and I hopped across. She started the car and we accelerated out of the parking lot.

"There's a shopping mall up ahead," she said.

At fifty floors, the Carlton Centre was one of the tallest buildings in the city. A few years earlier a property developer had bought it and turned it into the first high-rise shopping mall on the continent. It was a "destination mall". There were dozens of floors for fashion and home decor, but there were also floors for theaters, cinemas, restaurants, kids' entertainment, and more. People sometimes joked that you could go in there and never come out again.

"I'm not in the mood for shopping," I said.

Besides, the place would be a wreck, with all the looting and other savagery going on. Still, we cruised to a stop outside the main entrance and she clicked a button on her door to unlock mine.

"23rd floor," said Sugar. "Sports equipment."

Maybe the violence had gotten to Shagar, too. She wasn't making any sense.

"There's an archery section," she said. "Crossbows. Bolts."

I felt like hugging the mass murderer then, but I kept my arms to myself. "Thank you," I said, climbing out of the limousine. She gave me a flat-handed wave and gradually accelerated away, leaving me standing on the pavement, the massive Carlton Centre looming above.

OF COURSE, the elevator was out of order, and the lights buzzed on and off. Every now and then a bulb would explode and send my heart racing. Wild magic was definitely at play there. Dogs loped among the racks of clothes, cats sat licking their paws on cashier countertops. Potted plants, previously neat and manicured, had jumped out of their pots and sprawled across entire rooms. Broken glass glittered on the floor, and merchandise was spread all over the place, as if the looters had been interrupted mid-smash-and-grab. The spookiest thing about the place was the absence of people. Had every single untouched human been turned into a zombie?

I thought of Morgan and my blood pressure spiked. If she had been turned, I'd need to find a cure. I'd need to find out who was responsible for the possession plague and find a way to turn it around. I found the stairway and started climbing. At home I find it pretty easy to run all the way up to my apartment, and do it often to keep fighting fit. But right then it was past midnight, and my body was a mess of fatigue and nerves. A slow, steady jog was the best I could do.

I arrived at the twenty-third floor out of breath, my legs and lungs burning with exertion. The sports floor hadn't been robbed or damaged. I guessed the looters hadn't wanted to climb so far up, and, even if they did, they'd have little use for lycra tights and tennis balls.

I ran along the aisles, looking for the archery section, and soon a sign of a bow and arrow came into sight.

"Thank the Void," I whispered to myself. "Thank you, Sugar Shagar."

After ripping into some boxes and feeling like I was in a modern retelling of Goldilocks (too big; too heavy; too small; not powerful enough) I found a close-to-perfect crossbow. It was nothing like the one Ferra had designed for me, but it could fire a bolt, so it would do. I loaded it up and aimed at a mannequin wearing bright pink running gear, and pulled the trigger. There was a whooshing sound as the bolt left the flightpath, and it speared the dummy in the middle of the chest, knocking it backwards and making it clatter to the floor.

Happy enough with my new weapon, I strapped it to my back and put all the boxes of ammunition I could find inside my infinity pocket. Feeling the crossbow on my back and the weight of the bolts in my coat fortified me.

ON MY WAY out of the sports section I saw a poster with a map of all the color-coded floors. I wondered if I could grab a bottle of water. I was sure the restaurant floor would be a mess, but the camping floor might have something for me. The lights above flickered, hurting my eyes as I searched the map. I found the camping floor toward the top of the skyscraper, but noticed something even better just above it: the hardware supplies floor.

I took to the stairs again, and started jogging up. It was a weird feeling, being in such a huge space alone, and as I made my way up it felt more and more like a dream.

The home security section was everything I thought it would be, and more. I helped myself to a powerful Taser and some extra batteries for the flashlight. In some countries you can buy guns over the supermarket counter, along with your Marlboros and mints. In comparison, South Africa has stricter gun laws ... not that you'd think so from the proliferation of weapons on the streets. Still, I knew I wouldn't find a revolver there, but I did find a box of flares and a pistol. I tucked the flares into the pouch of my utility belt, creating a kind of makeshift ammo belt, and the flare pistol went into the outside pocket of my trench coat.

I felt bolstered, for sure, but I still didn't know where to find Morgan. I stood there, in the middle of the mall floor crowded with alarm systems and deadbolts and heavy metal house safes, wondering where to go next.

"I think I know who killed Liz Durison," Morgan had said over the line, crackling with static. *"I think I know who the V-Cult killer is."*

Morgan hadn't been taken from her home. She had left in search of the killer.

Killer, she had said. Singular. We had assumed the V-Cult was a group, because the women's bodies had been found in quick succession, and the attacks had been so organized. But Morgan had obviously found something that pointed to one person. I wracked my brain. I squeezed my eyes shut and tried to think of everything we had learnt about the case over the last fortnight. Had it only been a fortnight? It felt like forever ago when she had phoned me and told me that all the dead bodies looked like me.

I half expected Liz Durison to appear; a ghost in a gimp suit, swilling her favorite vintage of rosé, but I think she had given up on me. It was a shame, because I had some new questions to ask her. I knew she couldn't tell me who had taken her life, but we could have slowly laid the groundwork together to move forward, building the path that would lead me to Morgan and the V-Cult killer. There had been a lot of distractions which made me take my eye off the ball, but then and there, amongst the security lamps and rape whistles, only Durison's case mattered.

I heard a shuffling sound from the other side of the vast space. I ducked down to hide behind a shelf lined with civilian bullet-proof jackets. I tried to keep my breathing as quiet as possible as I squatted down, out of sight. I looked for the exit to the stairs. It was where the sound had come from.

Deodamnatus, I was fenced in.

I didn't want to fight. I just wanted to race down that staircase and get out of there. I thought that maybe, if I stayed crouched behind the shelves, the intruder would leave, looking for a more exciting floor to plunder. But the sound was getting louder. It was getting closer.

CHAPTER 35
UNLUCKY MANNEQUIN

I swallowed hard and tried to calm my heart, which was hammering away and causing the blood to rush in my ears. I crept along the shelf and found another display case to hide behind. My plan was to inch out of there slowly, in the opposite direction to the footsteps I was hearing. But the person wasn't moving slowly. He seemed to know I was there and actively seeking me out. I reached the next shelf, increasing my pace, but the person was right on my heels. I could hear him now, smell him. It wasn't a bad smell, it was just human. Not merchandise, not plastic or packaging.

I decided I'd have to run for it. If I was lucky I'd beat him to the exit. If not, I'd fight. I was scared, but the feeling of the crossbow on my back gave me a measure of confidence. I was about to dash when I felt a hand on my shoulder. I gasped and spun around.

At first all I saw was his blue uniform. He was a security guard for the mall, which explained how he had found me. He'd probably seen me steal into the store on one of the cameras. Before I had time to feel relieved that he was one of the good guys, I looked at his face. His eyes were silver and lined with blood. Small dark capillaries snaked out from them, reminding me of the way Slyden Abarim looked when the dark arts had taken over him. I gasped again and stepped away, upending a display column as I scrambled and fell backwards to the tiled floor. He reached for his gun.

There was no expression on his face; he seemed empty of emotion. He wore a snarl as if it were a mask that didn't belong to him; as if someone was controlling him remotely. A wireless puppet.

I glanced around, desperate, ready to reach for my Taser, but his finger was already on the trigger and he was squeezing. There was an eardrum-bursting crack of sound and light, and the bullet missed my head by an inch, only because I had rolled out of the way. I rolled back and grabbed one of the many cadmium yellow canisters beside me, flicked the catch and pressed down as hard as I could. A stream of pepper spray blasted the zombie in the face. He started coughing, but didn't let go of his gun. I sprayed again, then rolled away and sprang up onto my feet. Standing, I could reach for my crossbow. I grabbed it and pointed it at the man, but not before he let another round off, and the bullet bit me in the shoulder. The graphene of the trench coat protected me from the worst of it, but the pain still blasted through me, sending me back a few steps and making me drop my crossbow. I started coughing too, as the pepper spray made its way into my lungs and stung my eyes. The spluttering man pointed his weapon at me again and this time I round-house kicked his hand, sending the gun clattering to the floor and sliding out of view. I scooped up the bow and pulled the trigger, sending a neat black bolt straight into his chest, causing him to suffer the same fate as the unlucky mannequin before him.

I didn't waste any time clipping the crossbow to my back and sprinting out of there, but when I arrived at the stair-well I heard more people coming from below. I looked up toward the top floor. I didn't know what was up there, but I had nowhere else to go. I loaded the flare gun and hurtled up the final flight of stairs.

THE PLAGUE POSSESSION had been worrying before, but the untouched people infected by it had seemed harmless. Now it seemed that the numb way they were acting was just the beginning of the disease, and it had morphed into something far more lethal. Now they were masked soldiers in an army, killing anyone in their way. And there were hundreds of thousands of people in the city.

When you blew up the Venom Lab, Lysander had said to me the last time I saw him, *you forced their hand. They had to come up with a different plan,* he said. *And it's much, much worse.*

You didn't need an IQ over twenty-five to guess who was behind this plague. The Silvanos had realized that they didn't need to convert muggles one by one by getting them addicted to a drug and turning them into vampires. They didn't need an army of vampires to win the war; all they needed was an army.

I thought that losing the Hammerskin contingent would put a serious dent in their plans to take over the Realm, but now I saw the Hammerskins were inconsequential, because untouched humans outnumbered the Neo-Nazi orcs by fifty thousand to one. The Silvanos had found a way to control the humans in such a way that they had become killing machines. The kind of magic that it required was beyond anything I could comprehend. Where was it all coming from? It seemed especially dire to me as I ran up those stairs, my volt cuff rubbing against my ankle. I refused to feel sorry for myself, though. I had to find a way out of there and get to Morgan, and I needed to do it fast.

CHAPTER 36
WIZARD ON ICE

I was hoping the zombies below me in the stairwell would peel off on the home security floor, but no such luck. As I climbed, I heard them behind me, boots slamming down on concrete in a menacing tattoo. The air got colder the higher I went, but I didn't have time to stop and think how odd it was. When I smashed through the double doors at the top, it all made sense.

A beautiful white lake of ice took up most of the fiftieth level, and I paused and watched the vapor rising from the frozen water. It was an ice rink. The rest of the vast room was dark, which made the rink look like it was glowing white. I ran to the kiosk on the side, tripping over something in the dark and going sprawling, knocking the air out of my lungs. I heard the zombies arrive at the door. I jumped back up and kept going, parkouring up a handrail and jumping over the counter, landing well behind it. I wrenched my boots off and grabbed a pair of ice skates. I skipped back toward the rink, pulled the skates on, plastering the Velcro down to secure them. The shoe-change maneuver cost me thirty seconds, but I thought it would be worth it to have that advantage on the ice. The zombies were clumsy on regular terrain. If I could lure them onto the ice I'd have the upper hand.

Skates on, I pushed off and swooped toward the middle of the great white disc of ice. My skating was a bit rusty, but I soon got the hang of it again, and was able to push off into a quick pirouette to test my stability. It was good. The cold vapor coming off the ice felt good, and it had a calming effect. I stayed in the middle, but kept moving around, warming up the muscles I'd need to dodge and weave. If they had an advantage, it was that they were in the relative dark, and I was right in the middle of the room in a halo of white light. This meant they could all see me perfectly, and I was the proverbial deer caught in the headlights. I blinked and tried to focus on them, tried to get a headcount. But as soon as I had counted twelve, it seemed that another dozen appeared. Soon it looked as if there were a hundred of them, which I thought couldn't be right. No way they'd all march up here for a lone wizard on ice. Or would they?

They kept streaming in. Having skates on was one thing, but killing a hundred zombies was another matter entirely.

The first attacker stepped onto the ice, and began walking brazenly in my direction. On his third step his feet flew out from under him and he fell, hard, bashing his head as he did so. Red liquid splattered onto the white floor below him. A cut on his scalp.

So they do bleed, I thought. *They are still alive.* I wasn't sure whether to be relieved, or more scared. Somehow the idea of a living zombie was easier to swallow. There was a chance that the thousands of infected people could be cured; it wasn't too late for them. Also, I preferred the idea of being killed by a live person over a dead one, but that's just a personal preference. I'm weird like that.

A SECOND MAN braved the ice. He only took two steps before falling. I moved my legs, pushing off and braking, making sure I was as comfortable as possible on the skates. More of the zombies began to advance, but they all fell before they got anywhere close to me. After falling, they found it difficult to get up again, and they slid blindly into each other. I lifted my flare pistol, ready to shoot anyone who got too close.

A woman with silver eyes began to crawl toward me. She moved slowly on her hands and knees, inching forward on the slippery surface. It was a good strategy. I pointed the flare gun at her and pulled the trigger. There was a loud bang, and a bright orange comet left the barrel of the gun and rushed towards her, slamming into her. Orange sparks and smoke exploded around her head, and her body collapsed, dead, on the ice.

I looked at the pistol in my palm. It was my new *ignem exquiris.*

I hauled my eyes back to the main throng of zombies. The problem with having so many bodies lying on the ice was that they provided a non-slippery base for the others to climb over. Slowly, relentlessly, the attackers moved forward in waves, until they got closer and closer to where I was standing. My adrenaline painted my insides neon while I lifted the pistol over and over, shooting the flares at the zombies. Yellow, blue, army green, red, their heads exploded. The ice was no longer white but spray-painted with blood and the tint of the emergency flares. When the flares were finished, I tossed the pistol away and unclipped my crossbow.

They kept coming. Slipping, falling, jostling to get at me. I began to skate around the zombies that were able to reach me, releasing neat black bolts into their chests. I shielded my eyes and tried to look at the entrance. Surely there were no more coming? But there they were, cascading in like vultures at a kill site.

I understood then that my skating experience didn't matter. The shoes didn't matter. I could have survived fifty attackers; a hundred. But there seemed to be an infinite source of the silver-eyed attackers who wanted me dead. I didn't know how, but I had to get out of there.

I shot an approaching woman in a nurse's uniform, then a man in a suit. I looked around the room, trying to identify a way out. The windows had no handles. I could break one of the panes, but then what? The building was fifty stories stacked to the sky. My parkour skills were on fleek, but there was no adjacent roof to jump to.

A zombie grabbed me from behind. I dropped my bow and elbowed him in the stomach, then swung around and punched him in the throat. He went down, but grabbed my ankle, and I fell down on the hard ice, smashing my elbow and sending pain radiating up my arm. He reached for my face. I grabbed the Taser from my belt, shoved it into his chest and discharged sixty thousand volts.

Fiat fulgur!

Spell-slinging was a hard habit to break. The man shuddered as the hot current burnt through his body. He choked, let go of me, and rolled away. I looked up to see that more of them were coming. I raised myself precariously and grabbed my crossbow, shooting as many of the zombies as I could, then sped to the far end of the rink and jumped over the barrier, my elbow still glowing with pain. I hauled off the skates and ran barefoot to a window, smashing it with the blade of the ice skate. It took five blows to finally crack the glass, and another five to smash it out of the frame.

When I stuck my head out to look down, I felt dizzy. I didn't usually struggle with a fear of heights but I also didn't usually plan on climbing a skyscraper five hundred feet above the black city streets below.

Holeeeee, I was thinking. *Holy Faex. I was going to die.*

I could hear someone behind me, and that made my mind up. I'd rather hurtle to my death than die at the hands of the nightmarish army inside. I could imagine their blind hands all over me, seeking out my softest parts. Tearing me open, shredding me, bit by bit.

Death by a thousand cuts. Nope, nopity nope. No thank you, zombie muggles. No thank you very much.

I took one last look behind me and saw the multitude of silver eyes peering sightlessly back, and I jumped out of the window.

CHAPTER 37
BLACK OBLIVION

I landed awkwardly, on a ledge a few feet down. I bounced off it and began to fall again, but this time I grabbed onto the concrete ridge, clutching it with all my might. I looked straight ahead, into the gray concrete, and forced a few shallow breaths to clear the panic from my mind. I glanced around, trying to catch sight of something that would help me to slowly maneuver my way down. There was an identical ledge to the one I was holding a few feet below, but letting go to try to catch that one would probably be lethal. I didn't think the odds were in my favor.

The rough surface of the cement was taking its toll on my hands. It was like sandpaper, which was great for traction, but my skin was grazed and bleeding. The skin on my fingertips was tearing. I was slowly slipping, and I had nowhere to go.

The dark city was quiet below me. I could see the Void Fracture out of the corner of my eye. If I fell, the Chaos Jar would surely shatter, along with my skull. I didn't even want to know what the consequences of that would be, but I was pretty sure that my friends wouldn't survive it. In a way, it wasn't just me hanging there by the skin of my teeth. It was also Ferra, and all her children, including the Belore twins. It was Morgan, and SaltySnap, and Bron, and Lou, and Darick.

I slipped some more, and let out a scream. I couldn't help it. The muscles in my hands were giving up. I tried to force them to keep holding on, but they no longer had the strength. My left hand began to cramp.

Hold on, I told my body, which now seemed a separate entity to my mind. *Hold on. For Ferra, for Morgan, for Darick.*

But I slipped again, and I knew I was out of time. I was just hanging on by a fingerprint. I cast around one last time for something to grab on to, something to kick towards. I stared longingly at the next window across from me. It had a thin sill. It wasn't deep enough to give me any real traction, but it was something. The problem was that it was too far away. I had nothing to push off to launch myself towards it. It was not within reach.

Deodamnatus, I said to myself. *FML.* After all this. After everything. Was I really going to die like this? Falling to the ground outside a shopping mall, for *faex's* sake. And not only that, a "destination shopping mall."

Destination: Halloween Heaven. I could hear the sugared-up kids singing already. That creepy song from the Freddie Krueger films.

One, two, Freddie's coming for you.

Three, four, better lock your door.

Five, six ...

MY FINGERS SLIPPED, and I fell. Panic made me lunge for the next window, but I didn't reach it. I bounced off the ledge below. It cracked my jaw, blinding me with stars. I couldn't see, and I couldn't grab, and I went tumbling down in the dark night. It felt like I was falling into nothingness, but I knew that wasn't true. I knew to expect the lethal slam of the tarmac below. There was a terrible rushing sound in my ears, and then a swishing. My heart was racing, my lungs gasped for air. The Chaos Jar, with its beautiful blue lightning, was my final thought before the black oblivion took me.

CHAPTER 38
SHATTERED SKELETON

I woke up with a start, confused as hell. My jaw was sore, but the rest of my body seemed to be in one piece.

Where's the blood? I thought. *Where is the shattered skeleton?*

I began to wonder where I was. Not at the bottom of a skyscraper, smashed to bits. Not in a morgue. Not in Halloween Heaven. I blinked, and tried to look around.

I was alive.

With a shock I realized I couldn't move my arms or legs. Had I crushed my spine? Was I in ICU? But I knew that the hospitals were closed. Samantha Farzad had told me so. I felt something hard against my back. I was sitting in a chair. No, I was tied to a chair. And surrounded by stained walls and the stink of orc leather.

Before I could begin to work out what had happened, something moved behind me, right up against my head, and I yelled in fright. But it came out muffled and muted. I was wearing a gag. I couldn't see it, but I could tell it was grimy, and it smelled like vomit.

The thing moving against me was another person. Someone else had also been tied to a chair, and we were sitting back-to-back.

I tried to yell again, but it was hardly audible, and the stink of the cloth made me retch. I tried to squirm out of the rope that was binding me to the chair, but it was too tight.

Orc leather, I thought. *An orc leather tannery.*

The production of orc leather was one of the Realm's dirty secrets. Theoretically it was illegal to use orc skin to make leather, but it was an excellent product and fetched such a high price on the export fabric goods market, and brought so much money into the country that it was often over-looked. As long as the orc was dead to begin with, and not killed for his or her leather, the officials would often look the other way, or slap the offender with an eye-watering fine.

I thought of the poisoned wedding party lying at Alcazar. Maybe the Hammerskins would be useful to someone after all. Perhaps their tattooed skin would even fetch a higher price. Some countries liked exotic things like that. Neo-Nazi lampshades. Hammerskin handbags.

There was a sound off to the right, but it was out of view. The person at my back moved and yelled. Morgan.

"Morgan!" I shouted. "Morgan!" but it just came out as a groan.

Hope in my heart. Morgan was alive. She squirmed as I had done, and then gave up. I wondered what kind of danger we were in. What was the kidnapper's plan? For a horrified moment I imagined the person arriving with a sharp tool to remove our skin, but I pushed it out of my mind. Just because we were tied up didn't mean we were here to be flayed alive, did it? There could be a perfectly reasonable explanation for the rope and the gag.

AN ORC STEPPED INTO VIEW. A skinhead. I swallowed hard. The high one-dimensional lighting gave him a scary mask for a face. In his hand glinted a curved knife, perfect for peeling.

I shook my head and started to moan, and Morgan did the same.

"No," I was saying. "No, no, no."

His chin was wet with saliva, and his eyes were black vacuums. I could hear—and smell—him breathing. He walked up to Morgan.

"No!" I screamed, and I could feel her body vibrating in terror behind me. "No!" I shouted again, trying to break the bonds that held me to the chair. He held out the knife, and my chest almost exploded with the terror I was feeling. If I still had access to my magic, the emotions I was feeling then would have blown the whole tannery to smithereens. Instead, I sat there, useless.

"Pretty," the orc said to Morgan. I assumed he was holding the curved knife to her cheek, but I couldn't see it.

I fought against the restraints again, tears of frustration springing to my eyes.

Don't touch her! I was yelling in my head. *Don't touch her! Rather kill me.*

As if he had read my thoughts, he sidestepped and stood next to me, blade in hand. He held it to my face, and I felt the blade pinch my skin as it penetrated my cheek. I yelled in pain, but the sound was no longer muffled. He had snipped my gag off, and it fell to my lap. Warm blood ran down my cheek.

"How did I get here?" I asked. "What's happening? What are you going to do to us?"

I didn't expect the Hammerskin to answer me, but the questions spilled out, regardless.

"General," he said. "General will decide."

My stomach turned to stone. The teetotaling general had not drunk the wedding champagne. I imagined he was infuriated by his entire army being killed inside the fortress and planned to take it out on me. I stared at him while a vague memory began to surface. I was falling, falling, into nothingness, air rushing in my ears, when I had heard a swooping sound, a flapping cape, and suddenly my body stopped falling and I was locked into a warm embrace. Arms like steel held me tight and I fainted into the broad, warm chest of my invisible savior.

CHAPTER 39
LEATHER FACTORY

But why would Lysander bother to save my life just to bring me to this nightmarish leather factory? Was it so that the few remaining Hammerskins could exact revenge for the mass murder of their men? Lysander wouldn't do that, would he?

He's a vampire, the voice in my head said. *Vampires are cold-blooded heartless psychopaths.*

But Lysander had saved my life before, and I, his. He had respected me at a time when I didn't respect myself. It's like we had some kind of unspoken agreement.

Vampire and vampire-slayer.

We knew we were supposed to hate each other, but it never seemed to turn out that way. Although I should probably think about re-evaluating that, seeing as he had delivered me to the ruthless orcs who had every reason to want me dead.

There was a swish of a cape and I sat up straight, expecting to see Lysander and his turkey-carving cheek-bones. But instead, it was Demetrius, and I felt hopeless again.

"You," I said.

"You," he smiled, showing his fangs.

"Why am I alive?"

"You know why you're alive," he said.

They must know I have the Chaos Jar. I'm the only one who can remove it from my pocket.

I caught him looking at the tattoo on my neck.

"Hey," I said, and he blinked, reluctantly looking up, into my eyes. His black hair was slicked back, Count Dracula style. "Why Morgan?" I asked.

"The cop was getting ... too close for comfort," he said. "We don't need humans stumbling in and wrecking our very carefully laid plans. We're so close, now. So close to realizing our ultimate destiny."

I thought of the red hardcover book by Zolastaro. I remembered the illustration of the New Dawn throne, replete with orc leather seats.

"Morgan was investigating the V-Cult case," I said.

The symbol Demetrius wore as a diamond pin on his expensive-looking cape was the same symbol as Liz Durison was branded with. An upside down Anarchy sign. A "V" breaking out of a circle with a double line drawn through it. How did the serial killer tie in with the New Dawn?

"Morgan was getting close to the truth," I said. "When she phoned me she said she knew who the killer was."

"As I said, we don't need people like her around."

"And yet she's still alive." I said.

"We needed to lure you in somehow. We kept her as bait. But then—"

"—but then Lysander brought me in."

"Yes," said Demetrius. It came out as a hiss, as if he disapproved.

"You're going to kill us both," I said. "Or leave us to the Hammerskin general, which will have the same outcome."

"No," said the vampire, smoothing his hair back. "The order—unfortunately—is to keep you alive."

"Whose order?" I asked.

Demetrius looked surprised. "Acheron Baldassare, of course."

. . .

I TRIED to kick against the chair, but it didn't work.

Damn Demetrius, damn Lysander, and damn *faexing* Acheron Baldassare. I wish I had plummeted to my death outside the Carlton Centre. I refused to be taken to Acheron and made into some kind of house pet. It would be a fate worse than death.

Demetrius began moving in the direction of Morgan with a hungry look on his face.

"You stay away from her!" I shouted, as I felt Morgan squirm against me. She moaned through her gag. Demetrius looked at me, annoyed at the interruption, then crept further toward Morgan. His fangs were sharp, and faintly tinged with yellow.

"I'm warning you, you cretin," I said. "If you so much as touch a hair on her head—"

I rocked in my seat, using all the strength I had to break loose. I screamed with the exertion of it. It didn't put Demetrius off. His face was right beside ours, his copper crimson breath warm on my cheek.

"No!" I screamed. "No!" I was out of control. Hysterical. Desperate for my magic, desperate to stop Demetrius. My stupid hands remained spark-free as my emotions exploded. In a frenzy I shot up, pushing off the ground, trying to escape the binding. I lost my balance, and the chairs, with both of us tied to them, fell sideways to the stained floor. I heard a whack as Morgan's head bashed the floor, and she stopped moving.

"Morgan!" I shouted, but her body lay limp beside mine. I wanted to weep, but the adrenaline shooting through my body allowed no such comfort. Demetrius was not put off by Morgan's unconscious state. Again, he crept towards her, and again I shouted for him to stay away. I could kick and scream as much as I liked, but I knew that Demetrius was going to keep going for Morgan until he got what he wanted.

"Wake up," I said to Morgan, but I knew she couldn't hear me. Demetrius's face loomed over us, his handsome teal cape hanging from his shoulders. My terror sucked all the air from my lungs. He crouched down over her, and I could feel his weight against me. I could smell his deathly skin. Demetrius moved his head back and opened his dark horrible hole of a mouth, baring his fangs. Then his face came forward, and he sank his teeth into Morgan's neck.

"Wake up, wake up," I whispered.

CHAPTER 40
WHITE WAX CRAYON

"Wake up," said Darick. "Wake up."

I flinched, still scared and confused, trying to scramble away, but Darick held me tightly in his arms and shushed me, comforting me until my body understood it was safe. My head throbbed like a *filius canis*. When I opened my eyes, I was no longer in the orc leather tannery.

"That was quite a tumble you took," he said.

"What?" My mouth was dry, my voice croaky.

Where was Morgan? Was she dead? Or, worse, was she a vampire?

"I leave you alone for a few hours," he said, "and when I come back you're flying out of a window of a skyscraper like some kind of barefoot superhero."

Darick was at the Carlton Centre?

"Morgan?" I asked, my voice croaky. "Dead?"

I heard a nervous cackle and moved my head in the direction of where it came from. Morgan stood, arms crossed, very much alive.

"Demetrius bit you," I said. "You're a vampire."

Morgan unbuttoned the top of her white blouse and showed me her neck. It was perfectly unharmed.

Oh thank the Void, oh thank you, oh thank you, I thought. I started crying, and Darick held me close again, and I breathed in the scent of his body. They let me cry for a few minutes, and the ache in my throat subsided.

"What happened?" I asked.

"You were dreaming," Darick said. "It's normal."

"What's normal?" I said. "Normal for what?"

"Normal for coming back from the dead," said Morgan.

Darick looked into my eyes. "Not quite, but you did have us worried."

Morgan stepped closer. "Darick broke his arm, catching you."

I glanced down at his arm, worried.

"It's fixed," he said. "Don't give it a second thought. How are you feeling?"

"Headache," I said. "And happy to be alive."

"If you felt a kind of paralysis before, that's normal," said Darick.

I thought of the sensation of being tied to the chair.

"I was right next to you the whole time," said Morgan.

"I had such a bad dream," I said. "A nightmare."

"You almost died, Jax," said Morgan. "Standing on that ledge between life and death ... it's bound to bring up some scary stuff in your subconscious."

"I don't know what magic you used to slow yourself down during that fall," said Darick. "But it worked. We'd both be dead without it."

I stared at him. The volt cuff was still firmly attached to my ankle. My mind swirled with pictures and I couldn't figure out what was real and what belonged to the nightmare.

"Talk me through what happened," I said. "Pretend I'm five."

"I went back to your apartment," said Darick. "Gizmo was there, frantic. He wanted me to find you. I had the feeling you were in danger. He led me to the Carlton Centre, but before I had time to enter, you came flying out of that window."

"The zombies, are they real?"

"Yes."

"That's Acheron's army," I said. "That's why they were trying to kill me."

"Possibly," he said.

"After I destroyed the Venom lab, Lysander said they came up with a new plan to recruit the untouched."

"Some kind of mass mesmerization?" said Morgan.

"Something like that."

"And the Council," I said. "They're after me, too."

They both blinked at me. I understood that I sounded paranoid, but it was true.

"Where are we?" I asked, looking around at the clean white walls and minimalist design.

"My panic room," said Darick. "Your home is no longer safe."

With so many powerful enemies, nowhere was safe.

"It's chaos out there," said Morgan. "Everything's gone mad."

"It's snowing," said Darick, and I frowned at him.

"Really?"

I thought of the superstition we held as children at the Copperfield Institute, leaving a white wax crayon on our windowsills as we slept.

Darick passed me a glass of water, and I downed it all in one go. I had to tell them about Musubarin, the Council, and the Chaos Jar, but my mind was muddled and I didn't know where to start.

Darick let me go. "I've got something to show you," he said. "I'll be back in two minutes."

He left the room, and the door locked automatically behind him.

"This is a panic room?" I said. It looked more like a luxurious bachelor pad. If that was what his panic room looked like, I wanted to see the rest of his place.

Morgan widened her eyes. "I know, right?"

"What are you doing here?" I asked.

She looked at me and there was something in her eyes I didn't recognize.

"What?" I said.

"You'll be angry with me if I tell you."

"Never."

Morgan bit her lower lip. "I was following Darick."

"What? Why? I thought you were following a lead on the V-Cult case?"

She bit her lip again and looked away.

"You didn't think…" I practically choked on my disbelief. "You didn't suspect *Darick*?"

"Of course I suspected Darick!" she said. "All of a sudden this man with a vampiric name shows up in your life and—"

"Darick is *not* a vampire," I said.

"And seems totally obsessed with you."

Something flipped in my stomach. I wasn't sure if it was excitement or fear.

"Just try to see it from my side," she said. "So this guy rocks up out of nowhere. He manages to insinuate himself in your life—"

"He *saved* my life," I said.

On multiple occasions.

"There were just a lot of red flags, okay? He just happens to show up in your life just as those serial murders started. And has he ever really told you how he found you, or what he wants with you?"

That was true. If Morgan's and my roles had been reversed, I would have been just as suspicious.

"I got Chuck Winnow to hack into Darick's cloud. He had a locked file. Chuck unlocked it. We found hundreds of pictures of you."

"What?"

"And information. Where you lived, who your friends are, where you hang out."

The excitement morphed into a definite feeling of fear.

She grabbed my arm, making me jump. "But then I followed him from your apartment and watched as he risked his life to catch you when you fell. And he carried you all the way here, with a broken arm. And I watched him work on you for hours, healing you. Then I knew."

"Knew what?"

"I knew I had the wrong guy."

CHAPTER 41
COLD NAVY INK

I lifted my leg and showed Morgan my volt cuff.

"The only way it can be deactivated is with a Scorpion chip. I really wish Musubarin hadn't made you hand your badge in."

Morgan's eyes lit up. "Funny thing, that."

"Funny?" I said. "Hardly." I was suffering from a distinct sense of humor failure.

"It's funny that I ended up in law enforcement."

"What are you talking about? You're the best cop I've ever met."

"I just mean it's ironic. Because I've never been very good at obeying authority figures."

Hope rose in my chest. "You didn't hand in your badge?"

"To be fair," she said, "Moose's thugs hauled me out, kicking and screaming. There wasn't really an opportunity to stop at the front desk."

Morgan unzipped her jacket. She still had her uniform on, and from beneath the shadows of the jacket glinted her gold Scorpion badge.

"Have I ever told you how much I love you?" I said, not taking my eye off the badge. I felt like Gollum discovering my Precious. She unclipped it and I lifted my ankle, resting it on a transparent plastic chair. Morgan held her badge to the cuff, and the five tiny blinking lights shut off, and the cuff clicked open. When I took it off, the sense of relief was so strong I could have danced. I could have sung. But I didn't want to put Morgan through that so instead I took deep breath and hugged her. "Thank you."

I had felt so useless with that cuff on. A world without magic was so gray and two-dimensional that I never wanted to ever be in that position again. I'd actually rather die than be sentenced to a life without magic.

I had missed the sensation so much that I decided to sling a small spell. Just a simple one, so that I could feel the power in my body again, so that I could feel the sparks under my skin. I unclipped my wand from my belt and looked at it.

"*Illumino*," I said. I watched the tip of the wand closely, but nothing happened. *"Illumino!"* I said again. Nothing. I frowned at Morgan, who looked worried.

"Maybe it just needs time," she said.

"No," I shook my head. "It doesn't work like that. The cuff created a force field around my body, cutting me off from the Void. The cuff's off now, so it should be working."

Was there something wrong with my wand? I clipped it back and decided to use my hands instead. I aimed at the wick of a candle and stirred up all the emotion I had in my chest, funneling up and forcing it through my arms. I focused on the wick so intently that the rest of the room disappeared.

"Ignem exquiris," I said, clearly and precisely.

But despite my laser focus and the emotion coursing through my body, I didn't feel the force, and there was no fire. The candle remained unlit.

My world tilted and turned gray. I stumbled backwards and leant against the sofa. What had happened? What had happened to my magic?

Morgan saw my distress. "You almost died, Jax," she said. "Maybe your body is still recovering."

But I knew it wasn't that. I had been at Death's door before and I had still been able to cast spells. No, something was wrong. Something was very wrong. Dread turned my blood to cold navy ink.

"The last time I couldn't use my magic was—" and I blanched at the memory. I had to put both hands on the back of the sofa to steady myself as the implications revealed themselves.

"What's wrong?" asked Morgan.

"The last time I couldn't use my magic was when I was imprisoned in Slyden Abarim's basement," I said. "He had put an enchantment on the room that cut off my power."

"You don't think—" said Morgan, but I saw fear in her eyes, too. "You don't think that Darick's done the same thing?" She was pale, and her voice was shot through with nerves.

I looked around at the panic room. Before then it had seemed extra-safe: bars on the windows, multiple high-tech locks on the door. We saw the micro-camera in the corner at the same time.

"Why is there a camera *inside* the panic room?" wondered Morgan out loud. "Surely it should be outside, and the viewing screen should be in here."

I walked to the window and wrapped my fingers around the bars. The vertigo-inducing view told me that we were very high up. No one would be able to get in from outside. Were the bars to keep us in?

"I did think it was strange," muttered Morgan. "The clothes in the closet."

I moved over to the wall of storage space. The beautiful one-touch infinity closet opened smoothly under my touch, revealing a wardrobe of half a dozen neat outfits in various shades of gray. I unhooked one from the bar and looked at it. A cozy jumpsuit.

"That's your size, right?" Morgan asked.

Still clutching the suit, I turned to look at her. I felt the color drain from my face.

"This isn't a panic room at all, is it?" I asked.

It wasn't a panic room. It was a prison.

DEAR READER

Are you ready for the final book in the series?

Book 6: The New Dawn Throne

We hope you'll join us on the last adventure of Jax and co.

Happy reading!

JT Lawrence & MJ Kraus

ALSO BY JT LAWRENCE

FICTION

WHEN TOMORROW CALLS

• SERIES •

(Futuristic kidnapping thriller)

The Stepford Florist: A Novelette

The Sigma Surrogate

1. Why You Were Taken

2. How We Found You

3. What Have We Done

When Tomorrow Calls Box Set: Books 1 - 3

(complete)

URBAN FANTASY

BLOOD MAGIC

(complete 6-book series)

1. The HighFire Crown

2. The Dream Drinker

3. The Witch Hunter

4. The Ember Isles

5. The Chaos Jar

6. The New Dawn Throne

CURSEBREAKER

(complete 6-book series)

1. The Dusk Reapers

2. The Haunted Portal

3. The EverShade Ring

4. The Obsidian Castle

5. The Pick Pocket's Curse

6. The Eternal Betrayal

STANDALONE NOVELS

The Memory of Water
(steamy psychological thriller)

Grey Magic
(witchy magical realism)

EverDark

(urban fantasy)

SHORT STORY COLLECTIONS

Sticky Fingers

Sticky Fingers 2

Sticky Fingers 3

Sticky Fingers 4

Sticky Fingers 5

Sticky Fingers 6

Sticky Fingers: The Complete Collection:
Books 1 - 6: 72 Short Stories

NON-FICTION

The Underachieving Ovary

(memoir)

The Indie Author Game Plan

～